MYSTERY ON COBBETT'S ISLAND

Trixie Belden

Your TRIXIE BELDEN Library

Trixie Belden and the
MYSTERY ON COBBETT'S ISLAND

BY KATHRYN KENNY

Cover by Jack Wacker

GOLDEN PRESS
Western Publishing Company, Inc.
Racine, Wisconsin

0-307-21521-0

All names, characters, and events in this
story are entirely fictitious.

CONTENTS

MYSTERY ON COBBETT'S ISLAND

An Unexpected Invitation · 1

OH, MOMS, do you know what?" exclaimed Trixie as she dashed into the kitchen, letting the screen door slam behind her and almost knocking a lemon pie out of Mrs. Belden's hands.

Her mother carefully put the pie, piled high with golden meringue, out of the way in the pantry, and then, straightening her apron, she smiled fondly at her daughter and said, "Yes, I know what: Another step and you would have had no pie for supper tonight! Now, try to calm down and tell me what has you so excited that you'd risk ruining your favorite dessert."

Trixie pushed back the sandy curls from her damp forehead and, taking a deep breath, said, "Mrs. Wheeler has invited the Bob-Whites to the beach for ten days!"

"To the beach!" said Mrs. Belden. "How wonderful! Tell me all about it."

As she spoke, she brought over a bowl of cherries and sat down next to Trixie, who had collapsed into a chair at the big, round kitchen table.

Trixie popped a cherry into her mouth. Her eyes were snapping with excitement. "Well, the Wheelers rented a house on Cobbett's Island for weekends this summer, so Mr. Wheeler could go deep-sea fishing. Then last week he found out he has to go to Brazil on business, and he wants Mrs. Wheeler to go with him."

"Yes, she told me yesterday she hoped she'd be able to go, because she's never been to South America," Mrs. Belden said, "but she didn't say anything about the invitation."

"I guess South America is the only place she hasn't been, unless it's the South Pole." Trixie laughed. "She probably didn't mention the plans because they weren't definite until today." She reached for more cherries as she continued. "Anyway, the Bob-Whites were all up at the clubhouse this afternoon, trying to think of something to do now that school is out."

"Well, the Bob-Whites usually find something to keep them busy and stir up a lot of excitement, too," her mother commented. She smiled warmly.

"I know we do. I guess it all started when Honey and I found Jim in the Mansion. A lot's happened since then," said Trixie, reminiscing.

"It certainly has," agreed Mrs. Belden, "but get back to the invitation."

"Well, Moms, we couldn't seem to think of any new projects for our club, and we were all getting kind of frust—frusted—"

"You mean 'frustrated,' don't you, dear? You're beginning to sound just like Mart with those big words." Mrs. Belden's eyes twinkled with amusement.

"As a matter of fact, it *was* Mart who said we were all getting kind of frustrated and that we'd all better go up to Honey's house and have something to eat so we could think better. You know how food is usually Mart's solution to a problem." She giggled.

Mart, Trixie's brother, was fifteen, eleven months older than Trixie. He looked so much like her that he was sometimes taken for her twin. In the last year he had begun to grow so fast that his wrists always seemed to be hanging too far out of his sleeves, but he still had the same sturdy build as his sister, the same sandy hair and blue eyes. Mrs. Belden smiled, for well she knew how all the Bob-Whites loved to eat, not just Mart, although he was probably the most ravenous of the group. Only yesterday her cookie crock had been emptied when all seven members of the B.W.G.'s, as they called themselves, had stopped at Crabapple Farm on their way home from their last day at school before vacation.

Besides Mart, Trixie, and her oldest brother, Brian, the other members of the secret club were Honey Wheeler and her adopted brother, Jim Frayne, Diana

Lynch, and Dan Mangan. All lived near each other a few miles outside the small Westchester County town of Sleepyside-on-the-Hudson, and all attended the same junior-senior high school.

"Well, just as we were eating those yummy brownies," continued Trixie, "Mrs. Wheeler came in and said she had some news for us. Honey, who seemed just as mystified as the rest of us, asked her mother what it was all about, and then she told us! Can you imagine?"

"I think that's wonderful," said Mrs. Belden, "and I can see no reason why you and your brothers can't go, if—"

The "if" was smothered by Trixie's grabbing her mother and giving her a bear hug.

"Where *is* Mart, by the way?" asked Mrs. Belden. "And Brian? Where is he?"

"Oh, Brian's out in the barn working on that old rattletrap car he towed home yesterday. All we need is another jalopy around here! And Mart is still up at the Wheelers' talking about the trip. We knew we could count on *your* letting us go, but do you think Daddy will agree?"

"That was the 'if' I was about to mention," said her mother, "but I'm sure that, if this expedition doesn't cost too much, he will let you go."

"Oh, it won't cost much," Trixie quickly assured her mother. "Cobbett's Island isn't much more than three or four hours' drive from here. You have to take a ferry from the mainland, and there's fishing and sailing and a deserted lighthouse and. . . ." Trixie was off again. "And I won't need anything but my old blue jeans and those shirts we used for gym last year—and maybe a new bathing suit?"

The last item mentioned was more question than statement of fact, and Mrs. Belden, obviously surprised, said, "Why, Trixie, don't tell me you're interested in getting something new for a change. Is my girl growing up?"

"Could be," answered Trixie thoughtfully. "Of course, I don't know what I'd use for money. The yearbook and my class ring took all my extra cash," she added, her face clouding. "What *could* I do?"

Her question was left unanswered as she and her mother heard the familiar sound of the Belden Buggy as it turned into the driveway. The family station wagon had been christened the Buggy three years ago, when a queen bee had chosen its interior as a perfect place to swarm. It had taken Mr. Lawlor, the local bee authority, all day to capture her and put her in a new hive, where she was soon joined by her faithful followers.

Bobby, Trixie's little brother, who had been playing with his electric train in his room, came running down the stairs, out the door, and up the drive to meet his father. He was followed closely by Reddy, the friendly but undisciplined Irish setter, who was never far away from the little boy. Trixie brought up the rear.

Mr. Belden had scarcely stepped out of the car before his children had thrown their arms around him, and Reddy began barking a joyful welcome. "Now, what have my pets been doing on their first vacation day? I wish banks closed for the summer, just like schools," he said, "but when a bank closes it's a disaster, not a holiday."

"Gosh, Daddy, do they ever have to close?" asked Trixie.

Mr. Belden walked toward the house with an arm around each one. He explained that in the old days, before banks were insured by the federal government, they sometimes failed, and the people who had money in them lost all their savings. But now such a thing was almost impossible.

Trixie thought of her college fund of fifty-nine dollars and seventy-two cents lying safe and sound in the bank; then she sighed contentedly. Smiling up at her father, she said, "Do you know what?"

By now they had reached the kitchen door, where Mrs. Belden was waiting to greet her husband. Bobby, unconcerned about banks since his treasure of eight pennies was safely hidden in an old leather bag under his mattress, ran off to throw a big stick for Reddy to retrieve.

"That's just what she asked me, dear," Trixie's mother said, laughing, "and I must say you'll have a hard time guessing the exciting news."

"We won't make him guess," said Trixie eagerly, and she told him about the wonderful invitation. As she saw her father glance at her mother, she hastened to add, "Moms thought you'd say we could go."

"Well, I think my girl deserves a vacation, and the boys do, too. You've all worked hard in school this year and kept your marks up, in spite of all the activities of the Bob-Whites, and you've seldom been unwilling to do the things your mother and I have asked you to do."

Trixie lowered her head to hide the flush she felt creeping into her cheeks, remembering several times lately when she had been asked to help with the dishes or clean her room and she had answered, "Oh, do I *have* to?" or "Do you mean right *now?*" Housework she really detested, but she resolved to try hard to be more cheerful about such chores in the future. And when her father, on his way to the living room with his paper, planted a kiss on top of her head, her spirits quickly rose again, and she dashed to the phone to tell Honey that she and her brothers could go to the island.

Honey's real name was Madeleine, but, as a little girl, she had acquired the nickname because of her honey-colored hair, which she wore in a long bob, and because of a disposition that, despite ill health when she was younger, had never been anything but sweet. Honey was taller and slimmer than Trixie. Her eyes were hazel and beautifully soft. Since meeting Trixie and becoming a member of the Bob-Whites, Honey had forgotten her illness and was as active and healthy as any of the other members.

"I'm so glad you can all go," said Honey when she heard the news. "At least there'll be six Bob-Whites. Dan just called up to say he can't make it."

"Oh, jeepers!" exclaimed Trixie. "What's wrong? He's our newest member, and it's not fair for him to miss out on the fun again, the way he had to when we all went out west."

"Did you notice how quiet he was when we were all talking about the trip?" asked Honey.

"Come to think of it, he did seem kind of unenthusiastic, didn't he?" replied Trixie.

"Oh, he wanted to come badly enough, but last month, without anyone knowing, he applied to several camps for a summer job, and yesterday he heard from one of them saying they'd take him."

"But I thought Mr. Maypenny needed him to help on your father's game preserve," said Trixie.

"I guess Dan knew that job was just part of the experiment to see if he would straighten out after the trouble he got into in the city. Mr. Maypenny didn't *really* need a full-time helper," said Honey thoughtfully.

"Well, he's certainly justified Regan's faith in him, hasn't he? And to think he got a job all on his own! No one will ever have to worry about Dan again," Trixie said, and Honey heartily agreed.

Regan, the Wheelers' groom, was a likable, red-haired young man, who had, on several occasions, helped out the Bob-Whites. He always welcomed them whenever they came up to the stable, showing his fiery temper only when he felt any of them had been careless in caring for the beautiful thoroughbred horses in his charge.

Regan had lost touch with his sister, Dan's mother, years before, and the first he knew of Dan was when a judge in New York wrote him for help after Dan had been taken into Children's Court. Dan's father had been killed in an automobile accident, and later, after his mother died, the boy had felt there was no one who really cared what happened to him. He had become involved with a city gang. The judge finally agreed to let him come to live with Mr. Maypenny and work for him, so that he would be near Regan, hoping he might get a new point of view and a new start in life. The adjustment hadn't been easy for Dan, but when he finally proved to everyone that he had as fine a character as his uncle, the Bob-Whites gladly took him into their club.

The trip was the sole subject of conversation during supper. Trixie was eating her third piece of pie when she again thought about getting a new bathing suit. Of course, there was the money in her bank account, but that was for college and must not be touched. She could ask her mother for extra work, but she already got five dollars a week for taking care of Bobby and doing household chores. Now that she was fourteen, she felt she should no longer depend on her family for extras. She had about given up the whole idea, when she noticed her father pulling a letter out of his coat pocket. He pushed his chair back from the table and announced that he had received a letter from Uncle Andrew that morning.

"Oh, Daddy, hurry up and tell us what it says!" cried Trixie, who always looked forward to hearing from her favorite uncle.

"Well, he's fine, and so is everyone at Happy Valley Farm. He says he may drive out to see us this summer, but, in the meantime, he wanted to get Trixie a present for her graduation from junior high. He didn't know what you wanted, Trix, so he sent me a check for ten dollars. I was stumped, too, so I decided just to give you the money."

"Gleeps! Ten dollars!" Trixie exclaimed, her eyes shining. "Excuse me, everybody. I've got to run right upstairs and write Uncle Andrew. He's saved the day!"

"What crisis is my dear sister facing that she should need ten bucks so desperately?" inquired Mart in his most sarcastic tone.

"Oh, you wouldn't understand, lame-brain," Trixie called over her shoulder as she dashed up to her room.

"Now, don't tease your sister, Mart. She just decided she has to have a new bathing suit," said Mrs. Belden as she started to clear the table. "That's all."

"That's *all!*" shrieked Mart. "That's the biggest news since Edison discovered the telephone."

"Or since Alexander Graham Bell invented radium," teased Brian.

"Well, I guess our princess wants to look her best at Cobbett's Island," said Mr. Belden with a smile. "I just hope she gets a blue suit. It's my favorite color."

Foul Weather • 2

THE DAY BEFORE they were to leave dawned clear and bright, and Trixie could hardly wait until after breakfast to phone Honey to get the latest plans for the trip.

"We're leaving early tomorrow morning," Honey said, "because it'll take at least three hours to get down there, and we don't want to waste any time. After all, we only have ten days."

"Jeepers, Honey, that's three days more than a week, and you know how much can happen in seven days! Remember our trip to Iowa?"

"I'll never forget that week," answered Honey. "But don't be disappointed if we don't find any mysteries this time to 'challenge our intuitive powers,' as Mart would say. Dad says Cobbett's Island is a very quiet place and hasn't had any real excitement for years and years. No mysteries there."

"Well, honestly, Honey, after the way I've been working in school this year, I'll be glad just to lie on the beach and relax." Trixie sighed.

"That'll really be the day, when *you* relax! Are you sure you can get ready by tomorrow?" Honey asked.

"I'm sure I can if I hurry," answered Trixie. "All I have to pack are my jeans and shirts and pj's and stuff like that, or should I bring a dress, too?"

"You just might need one," Honey replied. "I told Di to bring that pretty lavender one that brings out the purple in her eyes."

Diana had always been considered the prettiest girl in her class, with long, dark hair and large eyes that were sometimes deep blue and sometimes almost purple. She had joined the Bob-Whites a short time before Dan. Although she was somewhat quieter than Trixie and Honey, she had fitted easily into the club. She had twin brothers and twin sisters, but since they were much younger, she had welcomed a chance to be with a group her own age.

"I guess I'll bring that flowered print," said Trixie. "It'll pack easily. Now I've got to run. Moms is taking me to White Plains to get a new bathing suit. That old thing I had last summer looks like a rag."

"What? *You* are going shopping? Why, Trixie Belden, what's happened?" Honey fairly squealed with amazement.

"Oh, nothing much, except I figure if we're going to

the shore, I'd better not turn up looking like a beach-comber."

"Well, I never thought I'd live to see the day when you cared *what* you had on, but if you're really serious, try that new store on Main Street. I've heard that it's fabulous. We'll pick you up at seven thirty. Miss Trask is driving us down in the station wagon. Tom and Celia are leaving today, with the cook, to get everything ready. Call me when you get home from White Plains, Trix."

Miss Trask had originally come to the Wheelers as a governess. She was a good-looking, middle-aged woman with crisp gray hair, and her blue eyes were usually smiling. She had been a teacher in a private school Honey had attended, and when the Wheelers decided to buy the Manor House so Honey could live in the country, Miss Trask had been asked to come to live with them. Later, after Honey had persuaded her parents to let her go to public school, Miss Trask, whom everyone adored, stayed on to manage the estate during Mr. and Mrs. Wheeler's frequent absences.

When she first met Honey, Trixie had been quite awed by the large staff of Wheeler servants, but she now accepted them as a natural part of Honey's way of life. Tom Delanoy, a handsome young man, was the chauffeur, and he was always ready to give the Bob-Whites a hand when they needed him. Celia, the maid, a pretty, cheerful young woman, had married Tom a

few months before, and they had moved into the
"Robin," the luxurious red trailer which Mr. Lynch,
Diana's father, had given them as a wedding present.
They, with the cook, Regan, and Mr. Maypenny, made
up the staff.

In White Plains, Trixie and her mother were both
delighted when they found a lovely powder-blue bathing suit in the store Honey had mentioned. It was very
flattering to Trixie, and the cut was perfect for her
young figure. "Not bad, is it?" she said as she slowly
turned around in front of the big triple mirror in the
fitting room.

"Not bad at all," repeated Mrs. Belden, smiling with
relief to see that her daughter wasn't going to be a tom-
boy all her life. "I like it a lot, and I know your father
will approve of your choice, dear."

The whole Belden family was up at dawn the next
day. Reddy seemed to sense the excitement and kept
running around the house, getting in everybody's way
and even refusing to eat the food Mrs. Belden put down
for him. In the midst of all the confusion, Bobby came
down the stairs trailing a well-stuffed laundry bag
behind him.

"I wanna go to the iling, too. I'm big enough, and I'll
learn to swim, too!" he cried. "See, I'm all packed." And
he began pulling an assortment of toys from the bag.

Trixie caught him up in her arms and gave him a warm hug. "Of course you're a big boy, and now that you go to school, you can go to the new pool and learn to dive and swim and everything. I'll miss you, Bobby, but someone has to stay home and take care of Reddy and feed the chickens and look after Moms and Daddy. I'll bring you a present when I come home. Now, will you please help me carry this big suitcase outside?"

"Okeydokey. See, I'm strong enough to carry it all by myself," he said, quickly forgetting his disappointment in his efforts to prove his strength.

"Here they come," called Brian as the Wheelers' big station wagon turned into the driveway.

Jim jumped out to help Trixie with her bag, and after the other luggage had been put in the rack on top of the car, he managed, by some unobtrusive maneuvering, to seat himself next to her on the backseat. Brian, Di, and Mart took the middle section, and Miss Trask and Honey sat up front. There was much shouting of good-byes and admonitions of "Don't forget to write!" as they drove off.

"I have a feeling that this vacation is going to be just wonderful," said Trixie as she settled back, "and as I said to Honey, I hope it will be a quiet one!"

"Well, that's what you may want, Trixie, but I've noticed that you have a strange way of stirring up excitement wherever you are," Jim answered.

And, sure enough, excitement began to brew before

the Bob-Whites were more than two hours on their way. After crossing the Whitestone Bridge and reaching the end of the parkway, they stopped at a roadside stand to stretch their legs and have a bite to eat. The radio over the lunch counter was turned on, and just as they were about finished with their food, the announcer interrupted the broadcast for a bulletin: A storm that had been raging well off the coast of Long Island and Connecticut had suddenly veered inland and was due to hit the mainland that afternoon. Small-craft warnings had been issued, and people were advised to take precautions against heavy winds and tides.

"Gleeps," said Trixie worriedly, "we'd better get going before it hits the island!"

"I'm wondering if we ought to turn back," added Miss Trask apprehensively. But she was soon overruled by all six Bob-Whites, who pointed out that it wasn't even raining yet and they had only fifty miles to go. Their arguments seemed reasonable, so everyone hurried out to the car and piled in.

As they drove east, they noticed that the wind was picking up and the sky was getting darker and darker. Rain began to fall and was soon coming down in great sheets. Miss Trask, who was an excellent driver, had to slow down almost to a crawl because it was so difficult to see, even with the windshield wipers going at full speed. But after what seemed an age to all of them, Honey caught sight of a big sign. She wiped the steam from the window so she could read. "Cobbett's Island, three miles ahead. We're almost there," she cried excitedly. Everyone was so tense that nothing more was said until they reached Greenpoint, the town from which the ferry left. Miss Trask followed little signs through side streets leading to the ferry slip, and those sitting next to the windows began rubbing off the steam that had collected, eager for their first glimpse of the ferry. A big man wearing bright yellow foul-weather gear beckoned them to come ahead. Miss Trask cautiously drove up the ramp and onto the large, white ferry, which bore the name *Island Queen* on its side.

Jim expressed what everyone had been secretly thinking when he said, "Gosh, I'm glad it's a big boat. I was afraid it might be a kind of oversized raft, like the one they use to get across the Connecticut River up near Old Lyme."

"I'll bet this would hold close to fifteen cars," added Brian, "but it looks as though we were the only rash souls out today."

As they drove on board, the ferryman suggested that they stop near the middle of the boat so the salt spray wouldn't drench the car. When he came back to take the fare, he said, "I reckon this'll be the last trip we'll make until after the storm. The tides are gettin' pretty high, and we won't be able to get into the slip. You folks are sure lucky you got here when you did. I see from your license plates that you ain't from around here.

Down to the island for the summer?"

"No, only for a week or so," answered Miss Trask. "We're staying at a house called The Moorings. Do you know where it is?"

"Yes, yes," he replied as he took a long drag on his pipe, which the wind and rain seemed unable to extinguish. "That's the old Condon place. No one lives there in the winter, but it's rented every summer. One of the purtiest spots on the island—that is, on a clear day. Don't look like we'll get a clearin' for some time to come, what with this east wind blowin' and all." He looked up into the sky, where the gulls, buffeted about by the winds, were screaming their defiance at the elements. "Jest follow the road from the ferry on through town till you come to the town hall, turn right there, and follow Shore Road for about a quarter mile. The Moorings is a big white house. You'll see the sign out front."

"The sea isn't always this rough, is it?" Trixie asked him as the ferry, now under way, was repeatedly lifted by the waves and let down with a dull *thonk*, and the spray beat over the front of the boat.

"Land sakes, no. Usually the bay's as calm as a bathtub, with fair winds for sailin', but every once in a while we get one of these danged nor'easters, and then you've got to batten down the hatches and ride it out." Bent almost double against the wind, he walked away to prepare for the docking.

The pilot, who sat in a little tower high above the deck, slowed the boat almost to a standstill as it approached the dock, then skillfully let the wind and the tide carry it between the high pilings. As it hit the side of the slip, he stepped up the engine just enough to take the boat close to the ramp, where it was soon secured by heavy lines.

If anything, the wind was blowing harder than ever, and, as Miss Trask drove off the ferry and up the street, they saw that several trees had been blown down. At one point, heavy wires were trailing over the ground, and a crew of men was working to get them off the road. "I'll bet we don't have any lights tonight, by the look of those wires," remarked Brian.

"Never bet on a sure thing," Mart replied. "We'll be lucky to have a roof over our heads. Wow, I've never seen anything like this in my life!"

"There's the town hall, I think," announced Trixie, who had her nose pressed against the window, "and there's a street off to the right. I can't make out the name, but I'm sure it's the right one, because I can see water from here and the man said it was called Shore Road."

"You're sure right. You can see the water from here," Jim agreed. "It's right across the road up ahead! Can we get through?" He leaned closer to the window.

"I'll get out and wade in to see how deep it is," Mart volunteered, taking off his sneakers and rolling up the legs of his jeans as the car came slowly to a stop. It proved to be fairly shallow, but every gust of wind was driving more water over the road, so he hurried back, wet to the skin and breathless from the wind.

"It's a good thing you rolled up your jeans," said Brian with good-natured sarcasm. "You might have gotten them wet otherwise."

"The secret of my highly successful life is that I always think ahead." Mart laughed, shaking the water from his hair and face.

Miss Trask drove slowly through the water so it wouldn't splash up into the motor, and presently, ahead, they saw a big white house with two wide wings.

"That must be The Moorings," Trixie said. "Yes, I can just make out the sign on the fence," she added as they came nearer.

Miss Trask drove gingerly into the driveway and under an old-fashioned porte cochere, which gave them some protection from the storm. A toot on the horn brought Tom, in a black raincoat, followed closely by Celia. Their worried expressions changed to smiles when they saw that all the Bob-Whites and Miss Trask were safe.

"What happened to *you?*" Tom asked Mart as he noticed his soaked clothes.

"Oh, I swam across. I didn't trust that ferry!"

Everyone was full of high spirits after the tension of the trip, and when the luggage was brought in, Trixie said, "Honey, I'm dying to see the whole house. Mart, you ought to get into some dry clothes. Come on, everybody, let's explore."

Celia led the way upstairs from the entrance hall and showed them the rooms they were to occupy. The girls were in a suite of two large rooms with a pink tiled bath between. Each of the rooms had twin beds covered with candy-striped spreads, thick cream-colored rugs, and attractively painted desks and dressers. Flowered chintz curtains hung at the big bay windows, which looked out over the water.

"We'll have to draw lots to see who sleeps where," said Trixie.

"Or we could play round robin and sleep in a different bed each night," Di suggested.

The boys went on to explore the large room on the third floor where they were to sleep. It had a distinctly nautical atmosphere, for the windows, instead of being rectangular, were round like portholes. At the foot of each bed was an old sea chest with rope handles at the ends and the original owner's name painted on the front. All the beds were covered with practical gray spreads decorated with large blue anchors, and instead of rugs, there were mats of woven rope. On the white walls were pictures of sailboats. Jim noticed a brass wind gauge just outside that was registering gale force winds.

"Gee, this is great," said Brian, throwing himself

down on one of the cots. "Those rooms the girls have look like the Waldorf-Astorbilt. This looks like a place to be lived in."

He was interrupted by Jim, who suddenly asked, "Say, do you hear someone calling?" As they listened, they could hear through the roar of the wind what sounded like someone calling for help. The three boys ran to the windows, but could see no one, so they raced downstairs, calling out to the girls as they dashed past their rooms. They ran out through the front door, led by Jim. The girls followed.

An Emergency · 3

TRIX, YOU AND DI and Mart go around the back of the house, and the rest of us will go the other way. We'll see if we can find who was calling," said Jim when they all got out on the porch.

"Okay, and if anyone needs help, just whistle," Trixie said as they all dashed down the steps and off through the rain.

The Moorings was set in the middle of a large piece of land, fronting on the bay, which was just across the road. On either side of the house were well-kept lawns, now strewn with branches and leaves that had been torn from the trees by the wind. Flowering shrubs and shade trees had been planted along the sides of the house and near the high brick wall which surrounded the property. With Trixie in the lead, she and Mart and Di turned the corner of the house, then heard the cries more clearly. Rounding a large bush, they saw a man lying in the grass.

"Oh, you poor thing!" cried Trixie as she knelt down beside the stranger. "What happened? Where are you hurt?" she asked, for it was obvious that he was in pain.

"It's my leg. I'd just finished fastening a loose shutter up on the second floor, when the wind caught me and the ladder, and the next thing I knew I was down here. I'm afraid it's broken, because every time I try to get up or move, it hurts like the very dev—I mean, like the very blazes!" Despite his pain, he managed to smile up at Di and Mart, who were now anxiously bending over him. When Trixie realized this was an emergency, she gave a shrill Bob-White whistle, which brought the other three running from the opposite side of the house.

"It's his leg, Brian," Trixie said hurriedly. "It may be broken."

Brian, whose ambition was to become a doctor, quickly sized up the situation and took charge. He asked Diana to run into the house for blankets. "We'll need them to cover Mr.— What *is* your name, by the way?" he asked with a reassuring smile as he knelt down beside Trixie.

"Elmer Thomas, son," the man replied, "but everyone around here calls me El. I'm the caretaker. That is, I *was* the caretaker until a few minutes ago. I guess I won't be much good for a while now." He winced

with pain, and Brian noticed that his face was unnaturally pale.

"Don't you worry, El," said Trixie warmly. "We'll see
that everything is taken care of as long as we're here.
We're staying at The Moorings for a while with Honey
Wheeler."

"That's real good of you. I appreciate it," El said,
trying to raise himself on his elbows.

"Now, you just lie back, El, and we'll have you fixed
up in no time," said Jim.

Di was already in the house before Brian had had a
chance to tell her to get a doctor, so he asked Mart to
go and telephone for one. "There *is* a doctor on the
island, isn't there?" he asked El.

"There sure is, and a good one, too," El answered.
"Dr. Holmes has been here for years, but it won't do
any good to call. The phone's been out of order since
noontime. I tried calling my wife to tell her I wasn't
coming home until I got everything secured around
here, but the line was dead."

"Gosh," said Trixie, "in that case, we'd better send
Tom for Dr. Holmes. Mart, you go tell him, and ask
Celia to have the cook make some good strong coffee."

Turning her attention to El again, she heard Brian
say, "Now, the first thing to do is to get you into the
house and out of this awful weather, but we'll have
to be careful of how we move that leg, so there won't be
any more damage."

Di came running back with the blankets. She also brought a big umbrella, which she held over El's head and shoulders while Trixie and Honey carefully covered him. While the girls were doing this, Brian asked Jim to see if something could be found to use as a stretcher. After he had gone, Brian very gently examined El's leg to see if he could locate the break. Just below the knee he felt a place where the shin bone was bent in an unnatural way, and El gave a cry of pain.

"It's not a compound fracture, thank goodness," said Brian, wiping the rain from his face.

"What's a compound fracture?" asked Diana, her eyes wide with interest.

"It's when the end of the broken bone gets pushed through the skin," explained Brian. "Then you run the risk of infection setting in."

"How come you know so much, young fella?" asked El weakly.

"Oh, he's going to be a doctor"—Honey broke in before Brian had a chance to answer—"and he knows all about first aid and everything about medicine."

"Well, not everything, I'm afraid." Brian laughed, obviously pleased by Honey's praise. "But I do read a lot, and last winter I got hold of a book about fractures and how to treat them," he added.

Just then, Jim and Mart came back with an old door. "We found it in the barn," Jim explained. "Lucky for us!"

"That's just the thing, but before we move him, we've got to put on a temporary splint, so the broken bone can't wiggle around," Brian said soberly. "Honey, see if you can find a couple of pieces of wood to use as splints and some old cloths to tie them in place."

"Look in the barn," suggested El. "There should be some pieces of kindling in there and some clean rags I keep for painting."

Honey was off like a flash, proud to be able to help out in an emergency. There was a time when she might have fainted dead away when faced with an accident, but she had learned many things, including fortitude, from Trixie and the other Bob-Whites. She was soon back with two pieces of pine board and a handful of cloths. Trixie tore some strips and helped her brother put padding around El's leg. Then they put on the splints, one at each side, and carefully tied them in place.

"Now, all of you put your hands under El's left side and roll him over onto his other side so we can put the door halfway under him. Then we'll ease him all the way onto it," said Brian.

"No sooner said than done, Dr. Belden." Jim smiled. "Are you all right, El?"

"It feels some better with the splint on, but the pain's still there, for sure," the caretaker replied. "I don't know what I'd have done if you hadn't heard me call."

They lifted the door very carefully and, keeping

near the side of the house, where there was a little more protection, got El onto the porch and then into the house.

Celia met them at the door and suggested that they take the injured man into the library until the doctor arrived. She had built a cheery fire in the big stone fireplace, and, although it was June, the warmth was very welcome after the soaking they had all received. She soon brought two steaming cups of coffee for El and Miss Trask and told Honey that hot chocolate would be ready for the Bob-Whites as soon as they had changed their clothes.

"Yippee! Hot chocolate!" cried Mart as he dashed upstairs to put on dry clothes for the second time.

When they had all returned to the library, they found the doctor had already arrived and was examining El's leg. Dr. Holmes was a big man with graying bushy hair and shaggy brows. As he worked, he made gruff noises and said, "Hmmm, hmmm." He straightened up and scowled over the top of his horn-rimmed glasses, which he wore halfway down his nose. "And which one of you is responsible for this contraption?" he asked.

"I am, sir," said Brian in an unnaturally quiet voice. He had suddenly realized, when he saw the doctor's face, that he might have done everything wrong. Could it be that he had done more harm than good?

"Well, you're to be commended, young man. You have not only remembered to avoid shock by keeping

your patient as warm and dry as possible in this abom-
inable weather, but you have also put on a very passable
splint. If all the accident cases I get were cared for as
sensibly as this, my job would be a lot less complicated."

"Thank you, sir," said Brian earnestly, "but the others
did as much as I did."

"Well, it was good work," growled the doctor. "Now,
don't just stand around. Go get some of that cocoa I
smell, or you'll all have pneumonia. And you might
bring me a cup, too. I love chocolate." His eyes twinkled
merrily.

Trixie, who had at first been apprehensive, now realized that Dr. Holmes's gruff manner covered a kindly,
good-humored personality, and she hurried out to ask
Celia to bring him an extra-large cup of cocoa.

By the time he had finished drinking it, the fire de-
partment ambulance was at the door, and two men,
whom the doctor introduced as volunteer drivers, put
the patient inside and drove off to Dr. Holmes's office,
where an X ray could be taken. El managed a weak grin
and a little wave of his hand as he was driven away.
The doctor followed in a car that Brian estimated to
be at least fifteen years old, and, as he roared out of
the driveway, unmindful of the huge puddles, Brian
shook his head and remarked, "How can he ever get
that much steam out of such an old crate? He's sure
got it trained!"

After a late lunch, the Bob-Whites gathered in the

library again and spent the afternoon playing every kind of card game they could think of. They even tried throwing cards into an upturned hat; they declared Jim the world's champion when he succeeded in getting in all but two cards.

Then Mart took the cards and, with much elaborate nonsense, told everyone's fortune. "Aha! I see by these two black queens that two of us are destined to become famous detectives." He turned another few cards and added, "Yes, and they are both blondes."

"What's in the cards for *me?*" Jim asked.

"Very odd, very odd," said Mart, wrinkling his brows and studying the cards in front of him. "This shows a highly unorthodox situation. I see you are destined to be the head of a school for orphaned children, but I think it's going to be much more like a camp than a school."

"You're a marvelous fortune-teller!" Trixie giggled as she stretched out in front of the fire. "What a day this has been! I wonder how much longer the storm is going to keep up."

"All night, by the looks of things," said Di, peering out the window. "It doesn't show any signs of letting up. The water is almost over the bulkhead across the road, and the wind seems to be blowing harder than ever."

"Great start for a seashore vacation," said Honey despondently, for, as hostess, she somehow felt personally responsible for the weather. "Can't you think of something to do, Trixie, or shall we go to bed and bury our heads in our pillows for three days?"

"And not eat?" cried Mart. "Never! For goodness' sake, think of something, somebody, and quick!" Looking around the room with a mock air of desperation, he noticed a television set in one corner. "Even this is better than nothing," he wailed dramatically as he went over and turned the dial. Nothing happened; the screen remained dark, and there was dead silence. "The antenna has probably blown down," he said. "Anyone else have any brilliant suggestions for whiling away the tedium during our incarceration?"

Before anyone could answer, Celia came in carrying a platter heaped with huge steaks. "The electricity is off," she announced cheerfully, "so if you want to eat, I guess you'll have to broil your steaks in the fireplace."

"Wonderful!" cried Trixie. "We'll pretend we're cavemen roasting our prime dinosaur steaks."

"And I'll be the prehistoric genius who discovers catsup." Jim laughed as he took the platter from Celia. "Food will while away Mart's tedium, or I miss my guess."

"Some genius had better discover some light around here," said Brian. "It's getting darker by the minute, and it's not even six o'clock."

"I noticed some old lamps in the barn when we were looking for a stretcher," said Jim. "Perhaps they'll work."

When he had brought two of them into the library,

they found that, although the lamps were old, they were well filled with kerosene, the wicks had been trimmed neatly, and the chimneys were bright and clean.

"Someone must have been through this kind of weather before," said Trixie as she touched a match to the wick and watched the flame brighten. They got more lamps from the barn and took one pair to the back of the house. Another pair they kept to use at bedtime.

The fire had burned down to a bed of bright coals. Jim arranged the andirons to accommodate the grill that Tom had brought in, and Honey, using a long-handled fork, laid the steaks on it. While they were broiling, the Bob-Whites set places around the fire with the plates and silver Celia gave them.

"I think eight minutes on a side will be enough," said Honey, enjoying her role as cook. "That's what your father said when we had that cookout at your house, Trixie."

"Don't ask *me*, Honey," said Trixie, giggling. "You know how much I don't know about cooking."

"You can say that again," chimed in Mart, always ready to needle his sister, whom he really admired. "Her recipe for toast is to let it cook until it smokes and then scrape off the black!"

"Maybe she's not the best cook in the world, but you can't say she's not tops when it comes to solving really tough cases," said Jim, looking fondly at Trixie, who,

for her part, was awfully glad the heat of the fire
gave a good excuse for what she knew was a very red
face.

"Can we trust you to take steaks out for Miss Trask
and the others?" Honey laughed as she handed the
plate to Mart.

"Are you, perchance, casting aspersions on my
honesty?" asked Mart, sniffing the steak and rolling
his eyes in anticipation.

"No, we're just testing your willpower," Di answered.

"On my honor as a Bob-White, I won't touch it, but
you've got to promise not to start partaking of this
sumptuous repast until I get back."

"It's a deal," they chorused, "but hurry; we're all
starved!"

After eating her fill of steak, rolls, salad, cookies, and
glass after glass of milk, Trixie, who had resumed her
position in front of the fire, said, "I'll tell you what
might be fun. Let's see if we can find a good book, and
we'll take turns reading it aloud. There must be something here that will be interesting, although I must say
most of those tomes look awfully dull, if you can judge
by their bindings." She got up and started to browse
through the shelves, pulling out first one book and then
another. "How would you like to have me regale you
with *A History of English Criticism?* Or maybe you'd
prefer this fascinating volume on how to grow wine
grapes."

"Here's a possibility," said Jim, who had joined her. "It's Dana's *Two Years Before the Mast*. I know it's a true sea story, and it might be just the thing for a night like this," he added as he took the book over to the table to get better light.

As he riffled through the pages, an envelope dropped out. Trixie picked it up. "Jeepers," she said, "it looks like a letter, Jim." As the other Bob-Whites quickly gathered around the table, Trixie added, "Do you think we should read it? You know I can never resist investigating such things."

"Oh, this is so old it won't matter," said Brian. "Look how yellow the envelope is. Go on, Trixie, start reading it, and if it turns out to be a gushy love letter or something like that, we can put it back."

"All right, but I feel kind of funny about it," she said.

She pulled the letter out of the envelope and started to read it aloud.

The Neighbor · 4

DEAR MR. C,

" 'Tomorrow I leave again on the bunker boat. I don't know how long I'll be gone this time, but it really doesn't matter. The more menhaden, the more money, you know. As I told you, I'm worried! I know you said, when we talked last week, that I was being foolish, but I can't seem to help it. You've known me all my life, and you know the two big fears I've always fought against. I never could get the hang of swimming—guess I started too late—and the other thing is, I just can't bring myself to trust banks since Dad lost his savings back in '29. So if anything ever happens to me and I shouldn't come back, I've taken some precautions to save that thousand dollars Grandma left me. I want my boy to have it. You know where we always sit and talk? Well, halfway from there to the golden chain tree is

where I've hidden a chart that will show where the
money is. Several times I've thought about giving it to
you to keep for me, but I shied away from the problem
directly. Besides, I knew you would get some fun out of
figuring out another one of my charts. You'll know how
to read it, even if no else can, because of all the practice
we've had the last couple of years.

" 'If anything should happen to me, "start sailing,"
and when you find the money, please see that young
Ed gets it.

" 'Always your devoted friend,

" 'Ed'

"Well, for goodness' sake," said Trixie, looking
around at the other Bob-Whites. "What's it all about?
Is it a joke, or was there really an Ed?" Already she was
anticipating another mystery.

"When was it written?" asked Brian, leaning over
to get a better look at the letter.

"There's no date or address on it, and the envelope
just says, 'To Mr. C.' That's no help," Trixie complained.

"Read it again, and see if it makes any more sense,
Trix," suggested Honey.

When Trixie came to the words "bunker boat," Jim
interrupted to ask if anyone knew what kind of boat
that was.

"Never heard of one," said Brian. "Let's look it up
in the dictionary—must be one around here somewhere."

They all started looking among the large volumes on the bottom shelf.

"Here's one, right under our noses," cried Honey, pointing to a large book on a stand in the corner of the room. "Bring the lamp over so we can all see what it says."

"Jim, you hold the lamp," said Trixie, "and be careful not to tip it. We don't want any fires around here. Remember how awful it was the night Ten Acres burned!"

"I'll look it up," said Brian, opening the dictionary. Reading half to himself, he skipped over some of the definitions that didn't seem to apply until he came to *Bunker, n. [From MOSSBUNKER]: The Mossbunker. See Menhaden.*

"Well, that's a big help! Anyone know what a menhaden is?" inquired Trixie. No one did, so Brian turned to the dictionary again.

"Here it is," he said. "Um. Let's see now. It says the word is of Algonquin origin. 'A marine fish of the family *Clupeidae,* having a large head, a compressed body, toothless jaws, bluish silvery scales, and attaining a length of twelve to sixteen inches. On the Atlantic coast of the United States it is by far the most abundant of fishes, where scores of millions are taken annually and used for bait or converted into oil or fertilizer. Called also mossbunker or bonyfish.' "

"That's it, all right," said Trixie, looking over her

brother's shoulder. "Bunker's short for mossbunker, and Ed apparently worked on a boat that went out to get the fish."

"That explains *that*, Sherlock Holmes," said Mart, "but it doesn't help much in figuring out who Mr. C and Ed really are."

"Or *were*," added Trixie, disregarding her brother's sarcasm.

"Well, personally, I'm too tired to even think straight right now," said Diana. "Let's all go to bed, and tomorrow we may have an inspiration."

"That's a good idea," agreed Honey. "I'm dead for sleep, too. Come on, everybody. Not even the wind, the rain, and a mysterious letter can keep me awake tonight."

"Now that you mention it, I'm tired, too," said Trixie, yawning, "and for once in my life, I'm going to bed and not think about anything, especially that letter." She paused and a faraway look came into her eyes. "But it sure makes you wonder," she went on softly, almost as if to herself, "doesn't it?"

Honey offered to sleep by herself in one room, while Di and Trixie occupied the twin beds in the other. As they undressed by the light of the single oil lamp, Trixie thought of how, just a short time ago, Honey had been a delicate, frightened little girl who had frequent nightmares as well as frequent illnesses and who would jump at the slightest unfamiliar noise. Now she seemed able to cope with any kind of emergency and showed no concern about the dark or the storm that was still raging outside.

"Nine o'clock and all's well," Honey called back when she had reached the other room. "I'll see you tomorrow morning."

"Good night, Honey. You're certainly the 'hostess with the mostest' when it comes to storms. Never a dull moment!" answered Trixie.

"What do you suppose it will be like tomorrow?" asked Diana, stifling a yawn.

Upstairs, Jim, Mart, and Brian were discussing the same thing. Brian noticed that the wind indicator showed the wind now turning to the northwest, even though it was blowing as fiercely as ever.

"I read somewhere that when the wind shifts around like that, it means it may bring better weather," said Jim, looking hopefully out of the window into the stormy night.

"You're undoubtedly right, professor," said Mart as he flung himself into bed. "It certainly couldn't produce more inclement atmospheric conditions than have prevailed today."

"For gosh sakes, Mart, do you always have to talk like a walking encyclopedia?" Brian asked half seriously as he turned down the lamp.

"Not really. I just like to flex my literary muscles." Mart chuckled. "Who knows? I may write The Great

American Novel someday. But now—sleep!"

Jim was the first to awake the next morning, and he tiptoed to one of the little round windows, opened it, and looked out. The rain had practically stopped, and the wind was certainly less strong than the previous night, but he was astonished at the appearance of the grounds around the house. Branches, big and little, littered every foot, and he saw that a huge tree had fallen across the driveway.

With some difficulty, he woke Brian and Mart. At first they were too sleepy to take any interest in Jim's proposal that they get dressed and start cleaning up the yard, but finally Mart's nose caught the smell of frying sausage wafting through the window from the kitchen below, and he leaped out of bed immediately.

"Jeepers, why didn't somebody tell me there was sausage for breakfast?" he cried as he quickly started to get dressed.

"Oh, that's not really sausage," said Jim, pretending to be serious. "That's just a powder that smells like sausage when sprinkled on the stove. It's my invention for rousing people who sleep through alarm clocks."

Mart threw a sneaker at him. Jim caught it neatly and jokingly refused to return it until Mart apologized. Mart grabbed his friend, and they rolled around on the floor until Brian finally got the shoe away from Jim and returned it to Mart.

"Hey, what goes on up there?" called Trixie from the

bottom of the stairs. "You woke us up with all your noise."

"Oh, Jim was just trying to prove that brawn is superior to brain," said Mart, "but I was able, through subtle and devious machinations, to quell his enthusiasm and restore order."

"Another sentence like that and I'll throw something heavier than a sneaker at you," Jim said as they came downstairs and headed for the dining room.

It was not as large a room as the one at the Wheelers' house in Sleepyside, but it was most attractive. The furniture was painted white, the chairs had bright coral cushions, and there was a coral and gray rug on the black-painted floor. Over the sideboard hung a beautiful old Chinese painting of a heron standing on one leg among tall reeds. In the center of the table was an attractive arrangement of seashells on a straw mat.

Honey rang the little brass bell she found at the head of the table, and Celia, looking very pretty in her trim blue uniform, came in with a tray of orange juice.

"I'm sure you'll be glad to hear the electricity is back on," Celia said as she served the juice. "The power company crews must have worked all night to restore the service."

"Well, it looks as though our work is cut out for us. The yard is a mess," said Jim, "but we told El we'd take care of things, so we'd better get at the job right after breakfast."

"Oh, it won't take too long if we all pitch in and help, and then we can start working on the let—" Trixie caught herself as she saw Jim shaking his head at her. Celia was just returning from the kitchen with a platter of sausages and a dish of hot corn muffins, and, much as the Bob-Whites liked her, they had decided long ago to keep the affairs of the club to themselves whenever they could.

"You were saying we'd have to start writing letters home, so our parents wouldn't be worried?" Brian asked.

"Yes," said Trixie, glad to be helped out of her predicament by her brother's quick thinking.

"Miss Trask telephoned Mrs. Belden early this morning," said Celia, "just as soon as the lines were repaired. She didn't want to wake you. She told Mrs. Belden we were all safe and asked her to tell Mrs. Lynch, so you don't have to worry a bit. The Wheelers had already left on their trip, but she sent them a telegram."

By the time they had finished breakfast, the rain had stopped. Bright patches of blue began to show through the scudding clouds. It was still quite cold, so they put on sweat shirts and the red B.W.G. jackets Honey had made for all of them and went outside to where the tree had fallen.

"Jeepers, I don't see how we can ever move that without a saw," Trixie said ruefully, looking at the large uprooted tree.

"Maybe there's one in the barn. We've found just

about everything else we needed in there. I'll go see,"
volunteered Honey hopefully.

"Good idea," Brian said. "I'll come with you." He
grabbed Honey's hand, and they headed for the barn.
They were soon back, however, with the only thing
they could find—a very small pruning saw.

"This thing is worse than nothing at all," moaned
Honey, dangling the little saw in front of her. "I *do*
wish we could do something. Tom won't be able to get
a car out of here until that tree's moved. And that will
take a long time."

At that moment, Trixie interrupted. "Do you hear
something over there on the other side of the wall?"
she asked, listening intently.

From the sound of branches being pushed aside, it
appeared that whoever was there was making his way
toward The Moorings. They listened closely, and presently over the top of the wall popped a boy's head. "Hi,
strangers. Are you castaways, or are you by any chance
from The Moorings?" he asked as he leaped over the
wall and landed in their midst.

"We're actually from The Moorings, but at the moment we feel like orphans of the storm," replied Trixie.
The others joined in greeting the newcomer. He was
as tall as Jim, with broad shoulders and a strong build.
His hair was so blond it looked almost white, and his
deep-set eyes were dark blue. He, too, was dressed in
jeans and sweat shirt.

"Gosh, that's great. Not that you're orphans, you understand, but that you're at The Moorings." He laughed. "I'm Peter Kimball from next door. I was hoping we'd have some life around here this summer. The people who rented your house last year were old. All they did all day was sit on the porch and rock."

"Well, there was certainly plenty of excitement around here yesterday," commented Trixie. "El, the caretaker, broke his leg just after we got here. We're guests of the Wheelers. Jeepers, I'm getting the cart before the horse, as usual," she said. "I'd better introduce everyone. Peter, this is Honey Wheeler, and this is Diana Lynch. This is Honey's brother, Jim. I'm Trixie Belden, and these two suspicious-looking characters are my brothers Mart and Brian."

"I'll get all those names straight before the summer's over. You *will* be here for the whole summer, won't you?" he asked hopefully.

"I'm afraid not," answered Honey, tossing her hair over her shoulder. "Just ten days. That is, the Bob-Whites will be here for ten days. After that, Jim and I may be coming down occasionally for weekends with our parents."

She had no sooner said this than she realized she had broken one of the rules of the club in mentioning it to a stranger, but as she looked around, she was relieved to see that the others didn't seem to be concerned about her slip. As they later discovered when talking it over, they had all taken an immediate liking to their new neighbor.

"The Bob-Whites, did you say? That sounds like a club. Am I right?" the boy asked with a smile.

"Well, you are, as a matter of fact," said Trixie slowly. "Of course, we're supposed to be a secret, or at least a semisecret, club, so if you tell anyone about us, tell them not to tell."

Peter and the others laughed heartily, and all agreed that, with all the members wearing identical jackets, it was rather difficult to keep the club really secret.

"But what does the 'G' stand for?" asked Peter as he examined the letters B.W.G. that Honey, who sewed beautifully, had cross-stitched on the back of each jacket.

"That's for Glen. We live near each other on Glen Road in Sleepyside. It was Jim's idea to call ourselves the Bob-Whites of the Glen," explained Trixie.

"I was in a club called The Owls before we moved down here. Not that we were wise or anything. We just liked to stay up late at night, and we spent most of our time thinking up reasons for not going to bed. It was crazy, but we did have a lot of fun. I miss those old birds," Peter said, smiling reminiscently.

"What do you do around here for excitement," asked Diana with just a suggestion of a flutter of her long lashes, "besides battling the elements?"

"I can answer that in one word: sailing! I'd rather

sail than eat," Peter answered. "As soon as the yacht club opens, I'm long gone in my Lightning. Do any of you sail?" he asked.

"Well, Trixie, Honey, and Jim here are pretty good hands with a rowboat," said Brian, thinking back to the time when the three of them had been caught in a flood in Iowa, "but I can't say any of us are actually sailors."

"I guess we've been too busy riding and fixing up our clubhouse and other things to think about boats," added Honey, "but it must be loads of fun."

"Did you say you sailed a Lightning?" broke in Mart. "Last Fourth of July there was a big regatta at Nyack, right across the Hudson from us. I read about it in the paper. I could see all the boats from the hill back of our house."

"I know. That was another fleet. But we'll have a regatta, too, later in the summer. Gee, you should be here. It's great!" exclaimed Peter, his eyes straying toward the nearby bay. "I was going sailing this morning, but I've got to get the mess from the storm cleaned up first. I was just starting when I heard you and decided to investigate."

"We were going to do some cleaning up here, too, but this tree has us licked," said Brian, giving the fallen trunk a hard kick.

"I should think so, if that's all you have to work with," said Peter, looking at the pruning saw that Honey was still holding. "What you need is a power saw. I'll get ours." He was off, over the wall, like a deer.

"Gosh, what a great guy!" said Jim.

"And did you notice what gorgeous eyes he has?" sighed Diana.

"I wouldn't say there was anything so special about his eyes," said Mart. "You squaws always flip for someone just because he has broad shoulders or gorgeous eyes or something. Don't you ever think about brains or character or anything?"

"When it comes to brains and character, we always have you, dear brother," Trixie flung back at him, "so allow us our little pleasures." Becoming serious again, with Peter out of earshot, she continued, "Say, you don't suppose, since he lives on the island, he might be able to help us with the letter, do you?"

"Oh, we weren't going to tell anyone about that," cautioned Mart. "For gosh sakes, Trix, don't always be so impulsive."

"I know, Mart," said Jim, jumping to Trixie's defense, "but he certainly looks like a dependable character if I ever saw one."

Stung by her brother's criticism, Trixie sat down on the tree trunk, cupping her chin in her hands. After a short pause, she said, "I suppose Mart's right. I know you can't always trust first impressions. Remember what we thought of Dan when we first met him? We were sure he was a crook, because he wore a black jacket and acted sort of antisocial. So it's okay with me to wait until we know Peter better."

"Good girl," said Mart, giving her a pat on the shoulder.

"All those in favor of waiting signify by the usual sign," said Jim, rapping on the tree, with a stone for a gavel. Everyone agreed.

Peter was soon back, and after he had handed the saw over the wall to Jim, he himself jumped over. "Now, this is more like it," he said as he got a firm foothold, adjusted the choke, and pulled the starter cord.

The saw made short work of the tree. Under Peter's direction, the boys took turns using it but manfully insisted that it was too heavy for the girls to manipulate. They had to content themselves with piling the big pieces of wood near the wall, to be split later on, and with taking the smaller ones to the rear of the house, where the fireplace logs were stored.

"Honestly," said Trixie, throwing down an armful of wood with unnecessary vigor, "boys think they know everything."

"Well, it doesn't hurt to let them *think* they do sometimes," replied Diana with a knowing smile.

The Letter • 5

It WAS WELL past the usual lunchtime when the lawn was finally cleared, but Honey had asked the cook to make a lot of sandwiches so they could eat whenever they got hungry. She invited Peter to stay for lunch, and he telephoned his mother to say that he wouldn't be home until later.

As they were eating, he said, "How about all of you coming over to my house? It's sort of interesting because it's the oldest house on the island. Would you like to come?"

"I can't think of anything that would be more fun!" exclaimed Honey. "I love to explore old houses!"

"Watch out for Trix and Honey, Peter. They're always exploring something and coming up with a mystery." Brian added, "Is your house haunted, by any chance?"

"Oh, there's some story about Aunt Cornelia coming back to try to find a lost fan," Peter answered, "but I never saw any signs of the old girl. Let's go back by way of the Shore Road. It'll be easier than going through the underbrush," he added.

They walked a short way down the road, then turned in at a beautiful wrought iron gate. As they were going down the long driveway, through thick woods where pink and white dogwoods were in bloom, Peter told them a bit about the history of the Oldest House, as it was called on the island. It dated from 1713, when Peter's ancestors first settled on the island, and it had been in his family ever since.

"Unfortunately, Uncle Jasper, who was the last to live here before we came, was a sort of oddball." Peter chuckled as he continued. "He wasn't interested in the house or the gardens, and he had just enough repairs done to keep things halfway livable. He spent all his time on some crazy research project. I think it was about the eating habits of some remote African tribe, but he never even got around to writing the book about it. So the place went to pieces while he lived here."

"What are those rocks over there?" asked Di, pointing to some crudely carved stones lying under a huge oak tree.

"That's a slave cemetery," Peter answered. "We found it last year when the tree surgeons were working on that old oak, and later, Dad found a list of the slaves who are buried there, written in an old ledger."

The driveway made a graceful curve a little farther on and revealed the house, set among stately trees and bushes of syringa and lilac. It was a two-story house with an enormous central chimney. The only thing about it that was not perfectly simple was the main doorway, which was dark red and flanked on each side by narrow leaded windows. Overhead was an arched panel bearing a beautifully carved eagle.

"Oh, how lovely!" cried Honey as they went through the gate of the picket fence. "I can hardly wait to see what it's like inside."

Peter called his mother, and she soon appeared in the large central hall to meet them and be introduced.

"I'm so glad to see all of you. It's always a pleasure to have Peter's friends here, and I want you to feel welcome at any time," she said with a warm smile that was very much like her son's. "And now, if you will excuse me, I'll let Peter give you what he calls the fifty-cent tour of the house. I'm trying to get ready for a garden party I'm giving later this week, but the storm has really put a crimp in my plans." With a friendly wave, she was gone.

"A garden party! What a perfect place for one," said Trixie, "but the storm sure came at the wrong time."

"I'll say it did!" said Peter. "We've been working for days to clean up the gardens, and we'd hoped to get the old gazebo in shape before the party, but I'm afraid now we'll have to let that go and just get this fallen stuff cleared up. I guess Mother will have to serve tea on the porch."

"Look, I have an idea," said Trixie, her eyes shining. "Why can't the Bob-Whites help you clear up? We haven't a thing planned, and we'd love to repay you for all the help you gave us this morning."

"I'm all for it!" said Jim. "How about it, Peter? When can we start?"

The others joined in enthusiastically as they crowded around Peter with suggestions and offers of help with the cleanup.

"Gosh, that's great of you. You really don't have to repay me for a thing, but this party is to raise money for a new town library, so, on behalf of the Library Building Fund Committee, I gratefully accept your offer," he said, making a theatrically low bow. "You know, if word gets around that more of the gardens have been opened up and the gazebo is restored, more people will come to see them."

"More people, *ergo*, more money," said Mart gleefully. "Right?"

"I don't know anything about '*ergo*,'" said Trixie, "but 'money' I understand. When do we start?"

"We can start as soon as I show you the rest of the house," Peter answered, leading them into the sitting room. He pressed one of the little rosettes on the mantel, and, to everyone's surprise, one of the panels above the fireplace slid slowly back, revealing a hiding place.

"There wasn't a thing in it except some old copies of *Youth's Companion*," said Peter. "Full of corny old stories!"

Beyond was the dining room, which was papered with some scenes from the days when whaling was an important occupation. The kitchen was in an ell at the rear of the house, and one whole side of it was filled with a wide fireplace and brick ovens. A refrigerator and modern stove had been built in so cleverly that the Early American atmosphere of the room had not been disturbed.

"What a wonderful place for parties!" exclaimed Jim. "I can smell the popcorn right now."

"As a matter of fact, we *do* usually end up here Saturday nights," Peter remarked.

After they had looked into the library, with its big mahogany desk, comfortable leather chairs, and shelf upon shelf of books, Peter took them upstairs to see a curious four-poster bed covered with a tester and with a trundle bed underneath. Each post was elaborately carved, and the bed was so high that one had to use a step stool to get into it.

They decided to postpone the visit to the attic until they had more time. Peter said his family had been so busy getting the downstairs redone that no one had had time to explore it fully.

"Jeepers, it's an awful temptation to start looking

through all those fascinating old trunks and boxes," said Trixie, poking her head through the narrow door that led to the attic, "but I know if we took one peek, we'd never be able to tear ourselves away."

"You're so right," Honey agreed. "Come on, everybody, let's get out of this enchanted house." She led the way down the narrow back stairs and out the kitchen door.

After getting rakes from a nearby shed, they took the path which led to the entrance to the gardens behind the house. It was obvious that the gardens had been lovingly and skillfully planned years ago, and even time and neglect had not been able to erase their beauty. Fruit trees lined a path leading to a shallow pool in which Mrs. Kimball had started water lilies. Behind the pool was an ancient statue of a woman holding an urn on her shoulder, and on either side were gracefully carved stone benches. Carefully laid out flower beds were already bright with color, and beyond them could be seen the vegetable gardens. To the right of the pool, and at some distance, lay the unrestored section of the garden. Honeysuckle and wild grapevines had grown to the tops of the trees, making an almost impenetrable tangle and practically concealing a little structure which Peter said was the gazebo.

"You know, I was wondering what a gazebo is," mused Diana. "I always get that word and carrousel mixed up, for some reason or other."

"My mother tells me these fancy little houses were the last word in Queen Victoria's day—for tea parties or just to sit in and gaze about. That's probably how they got their name," Peter offered.

They all went to work cleaning up the debris in the main garden, so that it, at least, would be presentable for the party, and it was dusk when they finally stopped work.

"If I can get everyone up early tomorrow, we'll be back and get this finished in jig time," said Trixie.

"Say, who was first up this morning, I'd like to know?" asked Jim with mock indignation. Turning to Peter, he continued, "I'll take charge of this work crew and have them here at eight, sir." He clicked his heels in salute.

On the way back to The Moorings, Trixie said, "Now how do you all feel about Peter and the letter?"

"Oh, I think he's about the greatest!" Diana answered with a faraway look in her big eyes.

Mart gave her a withering glance but agreed with Trixie that Peter certainly seemed dependable.

"How about you, Honey?" asked Trixie. "Do you think we should tell him about the letter?"

Honey thought for a moment and then said, "You know, anyone who loves old houses and gardens and will work like a beaver to make them beautiful must be all right. Personally, I'm for letting him share the secret."

The others agreed, and they decided to take the letter with them the next day and show it to Peter.

As it turned out, it was Peter who woke them the next morning. Miss Trask called from the bottom of the stairs that he was on the phone, and Honey, pulling on her pink dressing gown as she went, hurried to answer. Peter suggested that, since it was such a beautiful morning, they might like to go for a swim and then have breakfast at his house before getting to work.

Jim, Brian, and Mart, who had heard the girls racing downstairs, joined them in time to hear Honey answer in her sweetest voice that they would love to have a swim and would be right over. Playfully taking the receiver away from Honey, Brian asked Peter if the invitation included only the girls.

"You, too, of course!" answered Peter gaily. "You think I'm crazy? I'd never hear the last of it if Cap or the other guys saw me swimming alone with three beautiful mermaids. I'll meet you in front of our gate in ten minutes," he added, "so step on it!"

It didn't take them long to get into their suits, and, taking beach towels as well as shirts and shorts to put on after their swim, they set out for the gate of the Oldest House. On the way over, Jim, looking intently at Trixie, said, "Isn't that a new suit, Trix? Nice color." Without waiting for an answer, he dashed ahead to talk to Brian and Mart.

"Jeepers," Trixie whispered to Honey and Di, "he

actually noticed what color it is!"

Peter was waiting for them, and together they crossed
Shore Road to the sandy beach which ran in front of
The Moorings and the Kimballs' property. In contrast
to the last two days, the weather was now perfect, and
they were glad to see the beautiful island at its best.
Like Peter, all the Bob-Whites were excellent swim-
mers—Honey in particular. She ran onto the low spring-
board at the end of the dock and did a beautiful dive
into the clear, cool water.

"Good girl, Honey," called Brian. "You haven't lost
any of your form since last summer. Let's see you stand
on your head in the water."

No one except Peter had ever swum in salt water
before, and they were surprised at how buoyant it made
them. After a brisk game of tag, they began to get a
little chilly, so they came out and changed into dry
clothes in the little bathhouse at the edge of the beach.

Returning to Peter's house, they found places had
been set at an iron table on the brick-paved terrace. A
big pitcher of tomato juice was ready to be poured, and
while they were drinking it, Mrs. Kimball came out
with a tray of freshly made coffee cake and cocoa.

"Have you had breakfast?" Peter asked her. "Won't
you join us, or do you want us to save some of the coffee
cake for you later?"

"I know what all those questions mean, young man,"
Mrs. Kimball answered with a laugh. "They're just a

polite way of asking if you may eat all the cake and is there any more in the kitchen."

"Guilty, Mother." Peter grinned and passed the tray to his guests.

"I made a double recipe, and I've already eaten, so help yourselves," Mrs. Kimball said warmly.

"This is the best coffee cake I've ever eaten in my whole life," said Trixie. "Even Moms's isn't this good. May I have your recipe to take home, Mrs. Kimball?"

"Of course you may, my dear. It's one I found in an old cookbook in the kitchen cupboard, and what makes it so special, I think, are the black walnuts. We get them from a big old tree near the woodshed—that is, when we beat the squirrels to them."

"It's a good thing Dad isn't here," commented Peter, "or there wouldn't be a crumb left for us. This is his favorite breakfast, but he's gone up to Vermont this week to look over some properties for a ski lodge."

"Gosh, wouldn't that be neat," said Trixie, "to have your very own lodge to go to whenever you wanted?"

"Well, I could go whenever the Board of Education saw fit to give me a holiday." Peter smiled ruefully. "I still have to go to school, you know."

"I know," Jim said. "We never seem to have enough time to ski or skate at home, either. We don't have too many really good days of skiing in Westchester, anyway, and they never seem to fall on weekends."

"We aren't too far from Fahnestock, though," Mart

said, "so we drive up there when we can steal time
from our homework. They have a good ski lift and a
snow machine."

After Mrs. Kimball had returned to the house, Trixie
took the envelope with the mysterious letter out of the
pocket of her shorts, and, looking at Peter, she said, "We
have another problem, Peter. You were so good at helping us with the tree, maybe you can help us solve a
mystery." She handed him the letter, and Jim told
him how they had happened to find it in the old book.

"You see, we really don't know whether we have any
business reading the letter or trying to do anything
about it," said Diana seriously, "and since we're all so
new here on the island, we'd like your advice."

Peter whistled softly as he read the letter. "Well,
what do you know, a mystery right on this quiet little
island!"

"Trixie would turn up a mystery if she were marooned
at the North Pole," Mart chuckled.

"Do you think the letter is real—that is, do you think
Mr. C and Ed are real?" asked Trixie, ignoring her
brother's sally.

"Well, I don't know for sure, of course," Peter replied,
"but why would anyone put a letter in an adult's book
if it were written as some kind of joke?"

"Have you any idea who Mr. C might be?" asked
Brian.

Peter thought for a while; then, snapping his fingers,

he said, "Of course. How dumb can I be? The Moorings is sometimes called the old Condon place, because Mr. Condon lived there for many years before his death. He *could* be the Mr. C of the letter."

"Golly, I remember now," said Mart. "The man on the ferry said something about the Condon place when we were asking directions. I'll bet you're right, Peter."

"Could be, but that doesn't help much with 'Ed,' does it?" Peter said. "You know, I think it might help if we had a talk with Abe White. He's Cobbett's Island's one and only cop. Maybe he can shed some light on who Ed is. He's a good friend of mine, and we can trust him to keep this under his hat."

Mart turned to his sister and asked, "Did it ever occur to you, Schoolgirl Shamus, that maybe there *isn't* any mystery and that the thousand dollars has long since been found and given to Ed's boy?"

"Oh, I can't believe that," wailed Trixie, upset at the very idea of not being able to unravel another case. "I'll die if there isn't anything to it!"

"There she goes again," Jim said banteringly. "My co-president is frequently at the point of death, and it's only through the combined efforts of her loyal members that she is persuaded to face life again."

"Bear up, Trixie; we can't lose you now!" cried Honey with mock emotion in her voice, and everyone laughed, including Trixie.

"We'll go down at lunchtime and talk with Abe.

We can catch him at Bascom's store, where he usually eats lunch," said Peter. "I've just got my junior license, so we can drive down in the Icebox. That's what Dad calls my jalopy."

As they were stacking the dishes on the tray to take them back to the kitchen, they heard a noise of breaking branches in the nearby bushes.

"What was that?" asked Trixie apprehensively.

"Oh, probably a deer," answered Peter. "They get so tame around here that in the winter, when food is scarce, they come right up to the house. Or it may have been a tree that was almost blown down in the storm."

When Trixie got into the kitchen, she asked Mrs. Kimball if she had ever heard of a golden chain tree. "You have so many different kinds of trees here, I thought you might know about that one. I read about it recently, and the name fascinates me."

"As a matter of fact, we do have a golden chain tree —a very beautiful one. It stands just behind the pool. It isn't in bloom yet, so you wouldn't notice it particularly, but in a few weeks it will be filled with yellow blossoms which hang in panicles, or chains. It's a very old tree, and I think it's the loveliest one on Cobbett's Island. I wish we had more of them, but that's the only one."

The Bob-Whites listened to Mrs. Kimball with suppressed excitement. Here was another clue to the information in the letter. As she thought about the letter, Trixie instinctively put her hand in her pocket and realized she had left it on the terrace. She dashed back to get it and was surprised to find the envelope on the table where she had left it but the letter lying in the grass some distance away.

"Probably the wind blew it over here," Trixie said thoughtfully as she retrieved it, "but there doesn't seem to be a wind. That's queer."

The incident slipped from her mind, however, as she and the others went to work. Yesterday their work had been mainly picking up fallen branches and raking leaves, but today it was quite a different story. They found that the honeysuckle vines clung to the trees like demons, and the roots seemed to extend for miles under the soft earth. Together with the wild grapes, they formed a veritable jungle. But the Bob-Whites soon evolved a system for coping with the stubborn vines. Peter and Jim cut the main stems at ground level. Then Mart and Brian pulled the vines away from the trees, and the girls dragged them off to be burned when they had dried out.

Mystery in the Toolshed • 6

By NOON THEY had made good progress, but they were still not up to the gazebo itself. They decided to have hamburgers at Bascom's so as not to waste any more time than was necessary. After cleaning up, they piled into the Icebox and headed for the center of the island.

As they drove through the village, Peter pointed out the school, firehouse, and municipal hall, all of colonial architecture. "What's that ramshackle building over there near the school?" asked Diana, pointing to a dilapidated structure that looked completely out of place in the otherwise attractive center.

"That, my friends, is our library," replied Peter. "Do you see why we're so anxious for a new building? That one is over ninety years old, and while it was probably the pride and joy of the island in its day, it sure is an eyesore now. There are a lot of good books in there, even some rare ones, I guess, but who wants to go into a gloomy place like that?"

Bascom's was across from the school, and during the winter it was a favorite gathering place for Peter and his schoolmates. Today it was deserted, but Mrs. Bascom came bustling out of the back room and said she would be glad to make hamburgers for all of them. "I miss Peter and all the young folks after school closes," she said as she put buns on to toast.

As the meat was sizzling on the grill, Abe came in and, seeing Peter, called out, "Hi, Pete. What's new?"

"Draw up a stool and I'll tell you," answered Peter. He introduced the Bob-Whites to Abe and, after Mrs. Bascom had served them and was busy in another part of the store, told him about the letter.

Abe listened patiently; then, shaking his head, he smiled and said, "Personally, I think you kids are wasting your time. I'm fairly new on the so-called force around here, but I'd be bound to hear something about this if there was anything to it. Chances are it's just some directions for a treasure hunt. The summer folks used to have an annual hunt and went all over the island. My advice to you is to forget it. Don't waste your time."

"But don't you think—" began Trixie earnestly, but a nudge from Jim made her stop.

Abe finished his sandwich and coffee. Then, swinging off the stool, he adjusted the heavy leather belt that held his revolver, said good-bye to them, and left.

"I thought you'd better not say anything more to him," Jim explained, "because he obviously doesn't take any stock in the letter at all. If we talked about it too much, he might get the idea that we're prying into something that isn't any of our business and upset our applecart. As it is, he'll probably forget all about it."

"You're right, as usual, Jim," said Trixie. "We'll just keep quiet from now on. If there's anything to all this, we'll find out sooner or later."

"I'm glad we told him about it, anyway," said Diana. "Now we won't feel we're doing anything illegal."

"Well, let's get back to the jungle," said Brian. "We've got to finish cleaning up before we can do anything more about the letter."

As they passed The Moorings on the way back to Peter's, Trixie said, "Let's take just a few minutes off and see if we can figure out which building it is that lies between us and the chain tree."

"Okay," said Peter as he headed into the driveway, "but I'm afraid it isn't going to be as easy as it looks. Don't forget, the trees have grown a lot higher and denser since that letter was written."

"What was it the letter said about the tree?" Mart asked.

"I think it said halfway to the golden chain tree from the place where they used to sit," Trixie replied.

"How in the world can you tell where they'd sit, with

porches on practically every side of the house?" asked
Honey.

"Well, my powers of deduction lead me to conclude
that it couldn't have been on the west side of the house,
because you can't even see Peter's property from there,"
said Trixie, leading them around the house. "Let's see
what we can see from the other side."

When they reached the porch on the east wing, Jim
climbed onto the railing to get a better view. "If you
stand here in the middle, you can just make out the
chimney of the toolshed through the trees, but I can't
see the chain tree."

"It must be in that general direction, but we can't
tell for sure until we do a lot more clearing," said Trixie.

"We'd better get on with it, then," said Diana, and
they went back to Peter's and to work.

By dinner time they had cleared as far as the gazebo
and reluctantly called it a day. "We can easily finish up
in another half day," said Peter as they walked back
toward his house. "So what say we take tomorrow morning off and look through the toolshed? I'll bet anything
it's the place where the chart is hidden."

"I'm all for that plan. It will give my aching muscles
a chance to get back to normal," Brian said, rubbing
his back dramatically. "Football was never like this!"

"I don't hear the girls complaining. What's the matter
with you? Getting old?" asked Jim.

"Well, Mart and I were doing all the heavy work,

pulling those tough old vines down. All you and Peter had to do was cut them," Brian answered crossly.

"Oh, come on, everybody," said Honey. "We're all tired, and we're getting grumpy as bears. A good dinner and hot baths will revive us all—even you, Brian."

"Honey, you're wonderful," said Trixie, putting an arm around her friend. "You can always see what's making us out of sorts and come up with a solution. You're right; there's nothing like food to restore our spirits. So long, Peter, see you in the morning."

"And speaking of food, tomorrow we'll bring a picnic lunch to eat in the garden," added Honey.

As they started home, the sun was beginning to set, and as it sank below the horizon, the sky was aflame with constantly shifting rose and purple.

"Red sky at night, sailor's delight," said Trixie as they turned into their driveway. "Tomorrow should be another perfect day!"

The toolshed had originally been a summer kitchen, where, years ago, all the cooking and preserving for the family had been done, to keep the main house as cool as possible. Since the Kimballs had been living in the Oldest House, they had used the building for storing tools, screens, and storm windows. There was even enough space in the upper room for a kind of sail loft, where Peter could hang his sails to dry or store them during the winter months.

The next morning, when the Bob-Whites arrived, Peter showed them through the little brick building. When they reached the upstairs room, he noticed that some of the sail bags, instead of hanging from the wooden pegs along the wall, had been taken down and were lying in a disorderly heap in one corner.

"I'm sure I hung up all those bags last fall," said Peter, scratching his head. "I remember distinctly that when we took the boat out of the water after the last race, Dad helped me fold the sails, stow them in the bags, and hang them up. Now, who the dickens could have taken them down, and why?"

"Are any missing?" asked Trixie as she lifted one of the bags and read the words, HEAVY WEATHER MAIN-SAIL, stenciled on the side of the bag. "And this one next to it says 'heavy weather jib.'"

"You mean 'mains'l,'" chuckled Peter. "That's the way the old salts pronounce it."

"Aye, aye, Captain, 'mains'l' it shall be, and what do you call this one, a jib or a jab?" Trixie countered with a twinkle in her eyes.

"That's a jib. No problem there," Peter answered. "It's a smaller sail that goes in front of the mains'l, and here's the spinnaker," he said, pulling part of it out of the bag.

"Oh, what a lovely color!" said Honey. "Are they always blue like that one?"

"Oh, no. Cap's is plain white; some are red or yellow

or just about any color you can think of, even stripes.
It's quite a sight to see a lot of Lightnings coming down
the bay with their spinnakers up. Now, let's see," he
continued, turning his attention to the other bags.
"Here's the light weather mains'l with its jib, so nothing's missing. I don't get it," he said slowly as he
replaced the sails on their pegs.

Trixie, in the meantime, had been looking around the
room, and just as the others were about to go downstairs, she said, "Look, Peter. I've never seen you smoke,
but does your father?"

"No, Dad doesn't smoke, and I hate the things," he
answered. "Why?"

"Yes, that's a funny question, Trix. What's smoking
got to do with sails?" Jim asked.

"Only this. Look over here a minute. See all those
cigarette butts?" she asked, pointing to the corner.

"By Jove, what do you know!" exclaimed Peter as
he knelt down beside Trixie, who was examining them
closely.

"Trixie's found a clue. Trixie's found a clue," chanted
Mart.

"Maybe I have and maybe I haven't, lame-brain, but
I know one thing: There are only two brands here.
Whoever smoked this filter kind smoked his right down
to the tip, but the regular-brand butts are crushed out
before they're half gone," she observed as she separated the butts into two piles.

"There must have been just two people up here, then," said Brian.

"Elementary, my dear Watson," quipped Trixie, "and they must have stayed quite a while, judging from the number of cigarettes they smoked."

"Like overnight, maybe?" asked Mart.

"By Jupiter, you're right!" cried Peter. "And they probably pulled the sail bags down to sleep on. First I thought it might have been some of the little kids from school who think it's pretty smart to smoke. They know this place and might have come over to sneak a smoke, but they wouldn't stay a whole night."

"It looks as though someone wanted a real hideaway," Trixie said thoughtfully. "I wonder who."

"I guess we'll have to put a padlock on the door. We've never locked up anything around here before. The only way to get off the island is by ferry, so it doesn't make a very good place for burglars to operate," Peter commented. "Abe would have them before they could even buy their ferry tickets. They wouldn't have a chance."

"Couldn't anyone come and go in his own boat?" Diana asked as they went downstairs.

"Oh, I suppose they could," Peter answered, "but it isn't very likely. The mainland is much easier for a professional thief."

"Well, it certainly looks as though someone was prowling around here—someone who had no business to, professional or not," Trixie said solemnly.

"It's a funny coincidence that it should happen just after we found the letter, isn't it?" Honey commented.

"I wonder if it *is* coincidence," Trixie said, half to herself. "Let's look through this part of the shed and see if we come up with any leads," she suggested as she started systematically to examine the room.

The others joined in, but, despite an intensive search, nothing seemed to be missing or out of place. There was no sign of the chart's having been hidden there, either. No floorboards showed the slightest sign of having been tampered with, and even though they explored the old fireplace brick by brick, it revealed nothing unusual.

"Gosh," exclaimed Trixie, who had stuck her head inside one of the little ovens, "there's nothing in here but spider webs." She shook her blond curls, which were covered with dust and soot, and brushed the cobwebs from her face. "I don't think this is the place Ed meant at all. Oh, I'm so disappointed. Instead of finding the chart, all we came up with is evidence of an intruder whom we don't really want to be bothered with at all!"

"Oh, let's forget it. How about a swim to cool off? Last one in's a monkey's cousin!" yelled Peter as he dashed in the direction of the beach, with the others in close pursuit. They hurriedly put on their suits, which they had left in the bathhouse, and raced down to the water's edge. Peter was about to dive into the water when Trixie, who had managed to come abreast of him, grabbed him and pointed to a single sail out in the bay.

"Well, look who's out for a sail. That's Cap trying out his new Lightning. He's a top-notch sailor and a great guy," said Peter warmly.

"Gee, what a beautiful boat!" exclaimed Jim. "And he's sailing it all alone, isn't he?"

"That's one of the good things about a Lightning. One person can easily manage it, but in a race you have to have three people—the skipper, the spinnaker man, and a crewman who handles the mains'l."

"They must be awfully roomy boats to carry three people," commented Diana.

"Oh, they'll hold even more than that," Peter replied. "They're nineteen feet long and quite beamy, and—I'll tell you what," he said suddenly. "If we get the gazebo fairly well cleared out this afternoon, I'll ask Cap to take his boat, and I'll take mine, and we'll go for a sail tomorrow. How about going out to the abandoned lighthouse?"

"How perfect!" cried Honey. "Let's take a quick dip and then get back to work so we'll finish up for sure this afternoon. I've never been in a sailboat in my whole life, and I'm dying to go."

"Whoops! There goes Honey 'dying.' She's getting to be as bad as Trixie," Brian teased.

Honey chased him into the water, splashing him as she went.

"Let's race down to the dock at The Moorings and back," suggested Peter.

"Okay, any special stroke, or just freestyle?" asked Honey, who was the best swimmer of the Bob-Whites.

"Anything goes except a dog paddle," Peter told her. "On your mark, get set, go!"

Despite all her best efforts, Honey, who had been ahead at the turning point, was outdistanced by Peter on the return lap. "You're phenomenal, Peter!" she gasped as she climbed the ladder to the dock. "How do you do it?"

"It's a tricky little kick I learned last summer," Peter answered. "Come in again and I'll show you." They dived in, and after Honey had mastered the secret, she and Peter swam together in beautiful form. Trixie and the others clapped their hands in admiration as the two returned to the dock, shaking the water from their faces and hair. Then they all hurriedly dressed and ran back to the garden to have lunch beside the lily pool.

The Gazebo • 7

By FOUR O'CLOCK the lovely little octagonal gazebo had been freed of the encroaching vines. The original paint had begun to peel in places, but it was not in bad condition. The vines had probably served as protection from the weather, but the steps were quite rotten, and one of the delicate supporting columns was broken off completely. It was a great surprise when they uncovered a weather vane on top of the pointed roof—a copper boat under full sail.

"Isn't that darling?" sang out Diana, stepping back to admire it. "Do you suppose it works?"

"There isn't enough wind now to tell," answered Peter. "A little oil will probably get it going again if it's stuck."

While the others were talking about the vane, Trixie and Jim had been looking around the inside of the gazebo to see how much work would really be necessary to get it in shape for the party. Jim was examining the broken column, when he heard the sound of breaking wood and a cry from Trixie, and, turning quickly around, he saw that a floorboard had given way, and one of Trixie's legs had gone through and was caught in the hole.

As the others came running to see what had happened, Jim, who had caught hold of Trixie so she wouldn't lose her balance, yelled, "Peter, pull up the board next to this broken one, so she can get her leg out. Does it hurt, Trixie?" he asked solicitously.

"Not much," she answered. "It just stings a little around the ankle, that's all."

The board came up more easily than they had expected, and Trixie, stepping gingerly out of the hole, said, "That's funny. It doesn't look as though either of those boards had been nailed down."

"Oh, don't worry about the floor now," said Honey, putting an arm around Trixie's waist and helping her to one of the wide wooden benches built around the inside of the gazebo.

"Take a look at this ankle, Brian," said Jim as he knelt down in front of Trixie. A spot of blood on her sock was growing bigger, so Brian carefully took off her sneaker and sock. A look of relief came over his face when he saw that the wound was not a deep one but only an abrasion. Peter had already gone to the house for a first aid kit, and on his return, Brian carefully swabbed the wound with antiseptic and put on a sterile bandage.

"Lucky for us we have an almost-doctor in the house," said Mart. "Are you prepared to handle an emergency appendectomy?"

"Don't mention it!" chuckled Brian. "Don't think I haven't imagined such a situation. 'Brian Belden saves a child's life with a penknife.' Can't you see the headlines? The only hitch is that no one carries a penknife anymore, so my dream collapses."

"How long has it been since you've had a tetanus shot, Trix?" asked Jim as he was helping Brian put the scissors and extra bandages back in the box. "Do you remember?"

"Let's see. It was last year when I had my annual checkup. I loathe needles, even though they don't really hurt much, but Dr. Ferris said they're a lot easier to take than the treatment you get if you cut yourself or step on a nail and haven't been immunized."

Trixie, who was never one to brood very long about herself, again turned her attention to the hole in the floor. "We'll have to fix it before the party, and the steps, too. I wonder why those boards weren't nailed down." She knelt to get a closer look. Then she leaned way over and put her arm into the hole so far that her chin was practically resting on the floor.

"What on earth are you doing?" cried Di.

As Trixie drew her arm out, she brought forth a dust-covered bottle with the cork still in it.

"What's in it?" they all asked at once as Trixie carried it over to the seat and started to blow off the dust.

"It's awfully light, and it doesn't rattle, so there's probably nothing in it," she said.

"One of your ancestors was probably trying to hide an empty rum bottle from his wife," said Jim to Peter. "Here, let me have a look," he said, taking the bottle from Trixie. "Holy mackerel!" he cried, after he had wiped it off. "I think there's a paper all rolled up inside!"

"The chart, the chart!" cried Trixie. "Hurry and break the bottle and see if I'm right!"

"Oh, don't break it here. It'll get glass all over everything. Take it over to that rock," Honey suggested, pointing to a large stone, not very far away.

They all hovered around as Jim broke the bottle. Trixie picked up the tightly rolled paper and carefully spread it out on the ground.

"It's a chart, all right," said Peter. "Look; it has the compass marks up there in the corner. They call that a compass rose, and there's a black buoy and a red nun."

"A what? A red nun? I can't say that sounds very nautical," Mart said as he leaned over to get a better look.

"You're right; it doesn't," Peter answered, "but the red buoys are called nuns because they look something like a nun in her veil. They always have even numbers, so you say 'N two' or 'N eight.' Notice the harbor buoy the next time you're near there."

"What about the black ones? Do they have odd numbers?" asked Mart.

"Right you are," answered Peter. "They're flat-topped and carry odd numbers. They're called 'cans,' so you refer to them as 'C five' or 'C seven.' But what's that down there at the bottom of the chart?"

"Well, of all things to find on a map," said Honey as she looked over Peter's shoulder. "It's a bar of music!"

"A bar of music? That's funny." Brian was puzzled. "Maybe when Ed was drawing the chart he had a sudden inspiration to write a sea chantey or something."

"Well, he sure didn't get very far," said Mart. "Erato and Euterpe must have left him in the lurch."

"Who?" asked Trixie, for once falling into Mart's linguistic trap.

"The two Greek muses who preside over poetry and music," Mart answered loftily.

"Oh, no! You're not satisfied with English anymore. Now we have to endure Greek!" Trixie moaned.

"Here, Honey, see if you can make out the tune. You're our musical authority," said Jim, picking up the chart and handing it to her.

After studying it for a minute and humming softly to herself, Honey said, "It's just a simple bar of music, but it doesn't mean a thing to me. There isn't any time

indicated, and the notes are all whole notes. Listen."
She whistled the elusive little tune.

"Well, the main thing is that we've found the chart,"
said Trixie excitedly. "We were so busy cleaning up
this place that we never even thought the gazebo might
be the building Ed said was in line with the chain tree."

"Look; now you can see our porch from here," added
Honey, pointing toward The Moorings.

"Yes, and an imaginary line running from the tree
through the gazebo would end right where Jim stood
on the railing yesterday," said Trixie, her voice tense
with excitement. "Now all we have to do is follow the
chart and find the money!"

"Hey, not so fast," cried Peter, who had been studying the chart while the others were talking. "This isn't
going to be as simple as it looks."

"What do you mean?" Trixie asked. "It looks simple
to me, with all those landmarks, or rather seamarks,
on it."

"I know it does," answered Peter, "but the funny
thing is, it doesn't say where to start sailing. If you take
off from the dock at The Moorings, which seems the
logical place, and follow these directions, you end up
somewhere in the vicinity of our own cabbage patch!
Something's obviously wrong with that."

"Oh, bother!" cried Trixie. "Are you sure?"

"Let's all puzzle over it tonight, and maybe by tomorrow it will make some sense," suggested Diana.

"You were right yesterday when you said we should wait awhile, so I'll go along with your suggestion again," Trixie replied warmly.

"Maybe we'll get some leads on our sail," Peter said. "It may help us to see what it's all about when we get out in the boat. I think I'll make a copy of the chart, and you can take this one to The Moorings with you."

"Okay," agreed Jim as the Bob-Whites gathered up the tools and headed back to the shed. Peter drew the chart on the back of an old calendar that had been hanging on the wall, then walked as far as the gate with his friends.

"What time do you want to get started, and where shall we meet?" Trixie asked.

"I'll pick you up around ten—that is, if the Icebox cooperates. Sometimes she acts as though she resents my going sailing and refuses to start," he answered with a chuckle.

"If you have any trouble, call me up, and maybe I can give you a hand," Brian offered.

"Oh, Brian can make any car run, no matter how old it is," Honey said, looking admiringly at him.

"The Bob-Whites are full of hidden talents," Trixie added laughingly, "but when it comes to sailing, we are complete landlubbers."

"Don't worry. I'll give you the Special Kimball Sailing Course tomorrow," Peter assured them, "and by the time we get home, you'll be old hands!"

A Sailing Lesson • 8

IT WAS A FEW minutes before ten when they heard Peter's car chugging up the driveway, and they all ran out to greet him. Although the Icebox coughed and hiccoughed as it turned under the porte cochere, it *was* running.

"Should we bring sweat shirts or anything extra?" Trixie called out from the porch.

"It's a good idea to have something along to put on," Peter answered. "Even if it's boiling hot when you start out, it may turn cold, or the sea can get rough and toss a couple of buckets of water into the boat."

Celia came out carrying two baskets packed with food and handed them to Jim, who stowed them in the trunk along with the sail bags.

"Yes, Jim," Trixie teased. "You'd *better* take charge of the food and keep it away from Mart, or there won't

94

be anything left by lunchtime!"

They waved good-bye to Miss Trask, who had come out to see them off, and were away in a cloud of smoke from the exhaust.

As soon as they were on Shore Road, Trixie burst out, "You know, I had an idea about the chart last night just before I went to sleep, and the more I think about it, the more sense it makes."

"I'm glad someone had an idea," said Mart, shaking his head disconsolately, "because my cranial cavity was as empty as a broken drum."

"As usual," Trixie flung at him.

"Mother had so many things for me to do when I got home, I never did get a chance to look at the chart again," Peter confessed. "What did you figure out, Trix?"

"You know how clear it was last night," she began. "Well, I was standing by the window looking out over the bay, and I noticed a church steeple over in Greenpoint. It was lighted up with floodlights, just like the one back in Sleepyside. Later, I got to thinking it might be the one on the chart. Then I tried to remember where north is from there, and when I traced an imaginary line in the direction Ed had on the chart, it ended up at the yacht club."

"By Jove, Trixie, I believe you're right!" exclaimed Peter. "You have the makings of a crack navigator. I think I'll sign you up for my next trip to the South Seas. When we get to the club, we'll look at the big map and see if your theory makes sense."

Cobbett's Island Yacht Club was about a mile from
The Moorings by car. It lay almost directly across the
harbor from the house. It was an attractive, gray-
shingled building, surrounded by a fence made of heavy
chain supported by white posts.

After they had parked the car, they went inside and
looked for Cap, who Peter said had been delighted at
the idea of going for a sail with them. Cap wasn't in the
clubhouse, so they had time to look at the large map
of Cobbett's Island, the bay, and Greenpoint. Trixie
ran her finger slowly along the mainland coast and
finally found a circle with a little dot in the middle and
the word "spire" in tiny letters beside it. Peter, reaching over her shoulder, traced a line from that point
to the yacht club and compared it to the markings on
the chart, which Trixie had brought with her.

"By Jupiter, Trixie's right! The direction *is* southwest
from the church," cried Peter. "We'll lay that landfall
and go in as close to the shore as we can before heading for the next mark."

"You make about as much sense as Mart," Diana
said. "In plain English, what do we do?"

"I'm sorry," said Peter penitently. "I forget you're
new to all this nautical lingo. I meant we would head
for the church and then follow the chart to—let's see,
what is the next mark?"

"All it says is 'Rock,'" answered Trixie.

"It could be that submerged rock out there that they call 'Black Cat,'" Peter conjectured. "The big boats have to steer clear of it, but we don't have to worry about it in a Lightning, because it's so far underwater, even at low tide."

As they strolled around the glassed-in porch, they noticed pictures of beautiful yachts which had belonged to some of the club's older members. "This was Mr. Condon's sloop," said Peter, pointing to a large photograph on the wall. "It was a real winner in its day."

"Wouldn't Mr. Condon sail from here, then, if this is where he moored his boat?" Trixie asked. "I'll bet we're on the right track at last!"

"Come on, Trix, you mean the right course, don't you?" Peter chided her, with a laugh.

"Give me time, Peter. I'll learn," Trixie answered good-naturedly.

There was still no sign of Cap, so they continued to explore the club, going into a cheerful room with comfortable chairs, a big fireplace, and a cabinet filled with cups and pennants. In the rear was a hall, its ceiling covered with striped canvas giving the appearance of a huge tent.

"This is where we have dances, special events, and movies," Peter explained.

As they went outside and were walking toward the dock, Trixie said, "How about drawing lots to see who sails with whom? Is that all right, skipper?"

"Sure thing. It's a good idea. I was just trying to figure out how we might divide up," Peter replied.

Trixie picked up a pebble and a little scallop shell from the beach and held one in each hand behind her back. "The first three to pick the shell go with Peter and the others with Cap."

It fell to Trixie, Mart, and Di to go in *Star Fire*. The others would sail with Cap, who, at that moment, was running toward them down the dock.

In contrast to Peter, Cap was short and dark. He was solidly built, like a football player, and he carried himself well. His hair was dark brown and would have been curly had it not been cut so short.

"Cap, meet my friends from The Moorings," Peter said, "Honey, Trixie, and Diana. And these new deckhands are Jim, Brian, and Mart," he added with a smile.

"Sorry I'm late, Pete. Hi, everybody. Glad to have you on the island, even for only ten days. Pete told me all about you last night when he phoned."

They boarded a small powerboat operated by a young man in trim white trousers and shirt. Peter explained that the launch belonged to the club and was used to take members and their guests out to the boats moored in the harbor. "We'd never be caught dead in a motorboat ordinarily, but the launch is a matter of necessity." Peter chuckled.

"You can say that again," chimed in Cap. "No stinkpots for us."

As they came alongside Peter's sleek black boat, Trixie noticed its name, *Star Fire*, painted in gold letters on the stern. "What do you call your boat, Cap?" she asked.

"*Blitzen*—that's German for lightning," he replied. "And I can hardly wait to show old *Star Fire* here what a real bolt of lightning she is," he added with a wink to Peter. "*Star Fire* wouldn't have a chance."

Peter helped Trixie and Di step into his boat from the deck of the launch. Mart followed, carefully balancing one of the lunch baskets, which he had somehow managed to get away from Jim. Peter jumped in last, with the sail bags, and shoved his boat gently away from the launch.

"Let's go around Jenson's Point and then on out to the lighthouse," Peter said to Cap. "We can tie up and have lunch, if it doesn't take too long to get there. I see we're going to hit the incoming tide, and that'll slow us up, so if we get hungry before we reach the lighthouse, we can eat in the boat."

"I'm starved right this minute," moaned Mart, rubbing his stomach and rolling his eyes upward.

"After the number of pancakes you ate for breakfast, you shouldn't be hungry for days," Diana told him.

They waved to Cap and his party as the launch took them off to his boat, and then Trixie asked Peter what they might do to help him get ready to sail.

"Well, before we start anything, I'll give you the first

lesson," said Peter, looking a little embarrassed. "You see, the first rule on any boat is that no one does anything unless he is told to by the skipper. I know this sounds kind of bossy, but it avoids a lot of confusion." He laughed as he started to pull the mainsail out of the bag. "If I yell at you like Captain Bligh, don't think a thing about it; just obey!"

When they had put the rudder and tiller in place and hoisted the sails, Peter took his place in the stern and told Mart to unfasten the line that held the boat to its mooring. With Peter's deft flick of the tiller, *Star Fire* bore off, the sails filled, and they were away, making for the distant steeple.

"Don't worry if the boat heels," said Peter, "and I don't mean the way a dog heels behind its master. Heeling is our way of saying the boat is tipping on one side. All I have to do is let out this line, called the mainsheet, and the boat will level off and settle right down on her bottom. Heeling is a perfectly natural way for a boat to sail, so get comfortable and enjoy it."

"You mean the mainsheet is a rope and not a sail?" asked Mart.

"They say there's no such thing as a rope on a boat," Peter informed him, "only lines, guys, sheets, and halyards."

Cap was also under sail by now, and the two boats went out of the harbor with a good breeze blowing out of the west.

"See that red buoy up ahead?" asked Peter when they had left the clubhouse quite a distance behind. "That's the nun I was telling you about the day we found the chart. It's N two. When you leave a harbor, you always sail by the red buoy so that it's on your left side, or as we say, to port. When you return, you leave it on your right, or starboard, side."

"Whew! There's more to sailing than meets the eye," said Trixie, who had been listening intently to Peter's explanation.

"You can never learn all there is to know about sailing if you live to be a hundred," continued Peter. "Every time I go out, it seems the conditions of wind or tide or weather are different. That's what makes it such a great sport. It's just you and your boat, against nature."

"Say, Peter, that red nun we just passed doesn't show up on Ed's chart," Trixie said as she studied the map spread out on her knees.

"Could be it wasn't there in those days," Peter speculated. "Channels do shift, especially if there are heavy storms that change the shoreline." He looked behind him and pointed out a spit of land jutting out from the shore. "That's Jenson's Point over there," he commented.

"Aren't we going there before we go to the lighthouse?" Trixie asked, looking in the direction he was pointing.

"Sure thing," Peter answered, smiling, "but when you're in a sailboat, the quickest way to get from one place to another isn't always by going in a straight line."

"What do you mean?" asked Diana, wide-eyed. "Can't you just steer the boat like an automobile and let the wind push you along?"

"I wish it were that simple," Peter replied, "especially when I'm trying to beat Cap across the finish line." He explained that the boat isn't pushed along by the wind blowing against the sails, but that the wind flowing *over* the sails on the leeward side gives a lift, or suction action, that makes the boat go ahead.

"Sounds like the same principle as an airplane," Mart said.

"You're right," Peter answered. "As a matter of fact, it was through aviation experiments that they first discovered how the wind works. Men had been sailing boats for ages without really knowing how they operated."

"Leonardo da Vinci came pretty close to finding out way back around the year 1500," added Mart. "What a brain!"

"Now I see why you have to figure out where the wind's coming from, then zigzag back and forth to get where you're going," said Trixie.

"So we're actually going to Jenson's Point, even though it looks as though we were headed straight for England," Diana added with a giggle.

"Right you are," Peter answered. "We'll come about in a few minutes and tack in another direction, or zigzag, as Trixie said just a moment ago."

By now they were close in to the Greenpoint shore, where the spire was plainly visible. "Now we head for Black Cat, don't we?" Peter asked Trixie.

"We head for where Black Cat is *supposed* to be," she said. "Everything seems pretty elusive out here."

"Are those the bunker boats?" asked Mart, pointing to several large vessels tied up to docks on the Greenpoint shore.

"Yes, they're in port either to unload or for repairs," Peter explained. "They go out to sea for the menhaden unless the fishing happens to be good right here in the bay. Then you hear the men singing their work chants as they haul the nets. When they have a good load, they come back, unload, and pay off the men according to the weight of the haul."

"That's probably what Ed meant in the letter about it not mattering how long he was gone, I guess," mused Trixie. "He didn't want to come home until they had a full load."

She was suddenly interrupted by Peter. "Get ready to change course! When I holler 'Ready about—hard alee,' everybody duck, or you'll get clobbered by the boom. . . . Ready about. Hard alee!" he yelled, putting the tiller sharply over. All three crouched down as the boom came across, bringing the sail over to the other side of the boat. Then they all took turns handling the mainsheet and the jib sheets, Peter showing them how

to keep the sails filled by pulling in or letting out the
lines.

Trixie, when she had a free moment, spread out the
copy of Ed's chart again and studied it intently. Presently she said, "According to this, we've passed over
Black Cat Rock and should be heading south toward a
black buoy, but I don't see one anywhere." She shaded
her eyes and looked around in all directions.

"There's a black can a little farther on around the
point," Peter said. "That may be the one he means."

After several tacks, they came up close to Jenson's
Point. Mart caught sight of a blue heron just offshore
in the reeds, waiting patiently for a fish to show up.
Even though the boat came up close to land, it was so
quiet that the bird was not disturbed. The Bob-Whites
were curious about some tall poles along the shore.
They had little platforms on top, and on most of the
platforms there was a rough pile of branches.

"Those are osprey nests," Peter explained as a wide-
winged grayish bird rose from one of the poles and
screamed down at the boat sailing past. "Some people
call them fish hawks. They come up from Florida or
the West Indies in the middle of March and stay until
September. The telephone company put up those platforms for them so they won't build their nests on the
telephone poles and interfere with the wires."

"Or maybe listen in on our fascinating conversations,"
said Mart, laughing.

"One eavesdropping session on one of your conversations would cure them for sure," Trixie teased. "No bird, unless it's a wise old owl, could understand your language."

"Speaking of big words and ospreys," Peter said, "these birds are monogamous."

"Are *what?*" cried Diana. "Mart, do you know what he's talking about?"

Mart had to admit that he hadn't the faintest idea what the word could be.

"It means that ospreys keep the same mate for life," Peter told them, "and I've read that swans and geese have the same habit. Another interesting thing about ospreys," he went on, "is that they reinforce their nests before they go south, so they'll be in good condition in the spring, and even hurricane winds don't seem to knock them off."

Cap was now within hailing distance of the *Star Fire,* and, at Mart's suggestion, they decided to eat their lunch in the cove. They dropped anchor in the shallow water to keep from drifting, then hungrily opened the lunch baskets. The cook had prepared succulent chicken, fried to a golden brown, hard-boiled eggs, cucumber sandwiches, and brownies for dessert. A big Thermos bottle of orange juice was very welcome, for they were all thirsty after being in the sun so long.

"It's a good thing these eggs are already peeled," said Peter. "If there's one thing I hate to clean out of the

bilge of a boat, it's eggshells, and potato chips are just
about as bad."

After lunch Cap suggested they get under way, and
the two boats headed out into the bay, toward the
lighthouse.

An Accident • 9

PETER GAVE TRIXIE the mainsheet and asked Di to take
the jib. He shifted Mart, who was the heaviest of the
three, around to various places on the boat to maintain a
good balance. The wind freshened a bit as they got out
into the middle of the bay and headed east. Trixie,
glancing over her shoulder, noticed that Cap was tack-
ing, and she started to ask Peter why he didn't do the
same thing, but she remembered just in time what he
had said about the crew interfering and stopped in the
middle of a sentence, her face red with embarrassment.

"Don't be silly, Trix. Ask all the questions you want.
That's the way to learn," Peter reassured her. "Yes, I
see Cap's trying to put *Blitzen* around from the port
tack, but his sails don't seem to be filling very well on
starboard. Watch him! Whoops! There he goes, flopping
back to port." His voice was filled with excitement.

107

The Lightnings streaked through the water, spray blowing up over their bows, and everyone was tense with excitement.

"Wow!" Mart cried a few minutes later. "Cap's sure making up for lost time now. Just look at that boat go!"

"Come on, *Star Fire!*" yelled Trixie as *Blitzen* came almost abreast of them. There was much jovial shouting back and forth as the two boats raced for the lighthouse. When they came fairly close to it, Peter told Cap he was going in on the south side of the rocky pile on which the lighthouse stood, leaving Cap free to approach the old dock on the opposite side.

After dropping sails, Peter paddled around to the dock, using the one oar he always carried in the boat. While he did so, Trixie pulled out the chart again, mumbling to herself as she pored over it.

"Either Ed was crazy or we are," she finally said. "That last buoy just happens to be on the wrong side of the lighthouse. Otherwise, everything is dandy," she added sarcastically.

"Oh, Trixie, I'm beginning to think we're all wrong," said Honey, who had now joined her friend. "The rock didn't even show. The black buoy wasn't where it should have been, and now the nun has apparently walked around to the other side of the lighthouse."

"I know, but let's explore it, anyway. That letter was written ages ago, and, as Peter says, things change. It certainly looks as though the lighthouse is here where the chart is marked 'Finish,' doesn't it?" Trixie said with determination.

They secured *Star Fire* to the stern of Cap's boat, and Peter called out, "By Jove, Cap, that boat of yours can really move!"

"She did get up and go, didn't she?" Cap answered with a smile.

"She sure did, and she'll be real hard to beat," Peter replied. "The tune-up races are Friday, you know. So may the best man win!"

"Or the best boat," Cap laughed. Then, turning to the Bob-Whites, he added, "That's the funny thing about boats: No two are ever quite alike, even if they're the same class. Each has a nature all her own."

Peter and Cap had frequently visited the lighthouse, and they were anxious to show their friends through it. "It was built about 1890," Cap told them as they clambered up the rocks to the front entrance. "In those days, they got the light from oil lanterns with huge reflectors back of them. The keeper had to stay the year around to keep them going."

"I suppose electricity is more practical, but it sure takes the romance away from places like this," said Diana dreamily. "I'd love to live way out here, with a dog and cat for company."

"Oh, you know you'd get bored stiff after the first week without your friends," said Trixie. "You'd be inviting us all out to keep you company. But getting

back to the light, Peter, why don't they use the lighthouse now?"

"The sandbar gradually shifted, so the Coast Guard
put up the flashing light buoy to mark the channel."

Trixie had found time, while Cap was tying up his
boat, to tell the others that, although the chart looked
awfully dubious, they were all to keep their eyes open
for any clues. They went through all the rooms of the
two-storied house and up into the tower. All that remained of the building were the four stone walls and
the partitions. Vandals had broken the windows and
pulled down much of the stairway, but it was easy to
imagine the ghosts of past keepers still haunting the
place as the wind whistled through the vacant rooms.
But if the house held any secrets, it steadfastly refused
to give them up to the Bob-Whites.

After they had explored every nook and cranny,
they lay outside on the flat rocks in the sun until Peter
suggested they had better be starting back. "The tide
certainly hasn't been much help today," he said ruefully.
"We came out when it was going in, and here we are
going home with it dead against us. If we take the eddy,
we'll be back in plenty of time for supper, though."

"Hey, Pete," said Cap, "what say we each take a
different course home? You hug the island shore, and
I'll go over near Greenpoint, and we'll see if there's
any difference in the strength of the back eddy on the
two shores."

"I'm game," Peter answered with enthusiasm. "I've always had trouble deciding which was the fastest."

"What's all this talk about eddies?" inquired Mart.

"Well, let's see, how can I explain it?" Peter mused. "It's like shoving your hand in a jar full of water," he went on. "The water has to go somewhere, so it pours out from all sides. It's the same when the tide comes racing into the bay. You get a current along the shores in the opposite direction from the tide. Eddies help you to make better time when the tide is against you."

It was a perfect afternoon. The wind held, and as it grew later, the air cooled, bringing pleasant relief from the heat of the sun. They had been sailing for about an hour, keeping quite close in to shore, when the boat jammed into something, and there was the sound of breaking wood underneath.

Peter gritted his teeth as he pulled the tiller in an effort to maneuver the boat into deeper water, but *Star Fire* did not respond. "Here, take the tiller!" he cried to Trixie, who was sitting next to him. "Let all the lines go slack and pull up the centerboard," he yelled as he stripped off his T-shirt and dove over the side of the boat.

"What happened, Peter?" cried Trixie, voicing the distress they all felt.

"Do you want me to come in, too?" Mart shouted at the same time, but Peter was already in the water and could not hear them.

In a few minutes, which seemed like hours to the three in the boat, Peter grabbed hold of the side, and, pulling himself halfway up onto the deck, he said, "We've hit a big hunk of waterlogged driftwood, and our rudder's broken. It's lucky we didn't tear a hole in the boat!"

"Oh, no!" cried Diana. "I simply can't bear to think of anything happening to *Star Fire.*"

Peter shook the water out of his hair and climbed aboard. "Well, I can always get a new rudder," he said disconsolately. "It would have been awful to get a hole stove in her side."

Mart helped him lift the rudder off the rudder post and lay it on the seat. It was split right through the middle and, quite obviously, was useless.

Trixie looked to see if she could see *Blitzen*, but by now Cap was completely out of sight around the point. "Well, that's that," she said, half to herself. "What do we do, Peter?"

Peter noticed how Trixie had said "we" instead of "you" and exclaimed, "By Jove, you're really great!" The despairing look on his face changed to a smile. "A lot of kids would panic in a situation like this and yell for the skipper to do something, but here you are, cool as a cucumber, offering to help. That's really great!"

"Oh, we've been in lots worse scrapes than this and managed to survive," Trixie assured him.

"Neither wind nor storm nor hail nor a broken rudder

can stay us in the completion of our appointed task," Mart said, trying to look solemn.

"At the moment, our appointed task seems to be to get home," Peter chuckled. He decided to take the sails down and try to paddle back, using the one oar. He was doing all right until he reached a point where the force of the eddy slackened, and it soon became apparent that they were making no headway against the tide. In fact, the current was slowly but surely carrying them out into the bay and back toward the lighthouse.

"Mart, break out the anchor. If the water isn't too deep here, it may catch on the bottom," Peter said.

But this plan failed to work; the water was too deep for the length of cable on the anchor. Then Peter tied a line to the plastic bucket he carried in the boat and let it down over the stern. "This is one way to improvise a sea anchor," he said, "and it may keep us from drifting quite so fast."

As he worked, he kept glancing around him and finally said, "Someone will be coming along soon who will give us a tow, although there aren't many boats out this early in the season."

Trixie thought she sensed a note of anxiety in Peter's voice, although he was obviously doing his best to reassure them and to appear casual about their situation. "I'll hoist this red flag, just in case someone *does* come along. They'll see we're in trouble and not just fishing," he said as he produced a small red pennant from the drawer in the stern of the boat.

"Is that what the flag is for?" asked Diana.

"No, it's really a protest flag," Peter answered. "We use it during a race, when we see someone making a foul and want to enter a protest to the race committee. Actually, we don't often use it, but it's required equipment, and I guess it's lucky I followed the rules and had one aboard."

They were all on the alert for a passing boat, but the minutes ticked away without any sign of help showing up. *Star Fire* was being carried down the bay and, as they all realized, out to sea. Suddenly Peter's face brightened. "You know, I think if I use the paddle as a rudder, I may be able to steer us up to the red nun and we can tie up there. At least, it's worth a try."

He had no sooner put the oar in the water than they all heard the noise of a motorboat in the distance. A small yellow speedboat was plowing toward them. They stood up and began to yell and wave their arms as it approached, but to their amazement it kept coming at full speed, passed within a few feet of them, and careened away. *Star Fire* pitched and tossed in the wake of the boat, and Peter, trying to keep his footing, yelled, "You bums, that's just like a stinkpot!"

"Do you know those two characters?" asked Trixie, when she had gotten her breath.

"Never saw them before in my life," answered Peter, "and I don't want to again! Did anyone notice the number on their boat? They ought to be reported to the Coast Guard!" he added angrily.

"I'm not sure, but I don't think there *was* a number on it," replied Trixie. "All I saw was a dragon painted in green on the front."

The others agreed that they hadn't seen a number on the speedboat, either, only a green dragon with a long forked red tongue.

After the waves caused by the speedboat had subsided, Peter continued to edge *Star Fire* toward the buoy, and after what seemed hours, he brought her close enough for Mart to throw a line over it and secure the boat. They helped take off the sails and stow them in the sail bags, coil all the lines, and get everything shipshape in the cockpit.

It was growing darker, but they were all so relieved to be tied fast that they didn't immediately think about the problem of getting home. Peter, whose shorts were still wet from his dive into the bay, was beginning to shiver, so Trixie suggested he wrap his legs up in an old sweat shirt that she had found under one of the seats. They all put on the extra sweaters they had brought and prepared to sit it out until help arrived.

Peter started to sing a sea chantey. "Come, ye bold fishermen, listen to me; I'll sing you a song of the fish in the sea." There were endless verses, and the others soon joined lustily in the chorus. "Blow ye winds westerly, westerly blow. We're bound to the southward, so steady we go." He had a good voice and a seemingly endless stock of such songs, which raised everyone's spirits.

Mart rummaged through the lunch basket, hoping that something might be left from lunch, but there wasn't a crumb, and for once he refrained from mentioning his hunger.

The wind had died away as night really settled down on them, and a few stars became visible in the sky. Suddenly Trixie exclaimed, "I thought you said this was a flashing buoy, Peter! When does the light come on?"

"By Jove, Trix, you're right. It *is* supposed to be lighted," Peter cried. "The light flashes day and night, but, of course, in the daytime you don't notice it. Hand me the flashlight out of the drawer, and I'll see if I can find out what's wrong." He jumped up on deck, ran to the bow of the boat, and played the beam of light over the buoy. "The bulb has been smashed!" he exclaimed.

"Jeepers, what if a bunker boat happens to be coming in tonight? There won't be any light to guide it into the channel," Trixie said. "They'll be in a worse mess than we are. They could go aground!"

"Isn't there any way to fix it?" asked Mart, for once dead serious.

"Not a chance in the world," Peter answered in a low voice as he climbed back into the cockpit.

All four were silent, their fears rising as time passed

with no sound except the slapping of the water against the side of the boat.

Presently Trixie said, "Say, Di, do you remember that Christmas when we decided to go out to sing carols to the shut-ins, and we each carried a flashlight covered with red crepe paper to shine up into our faces?"

"Sure I do," answered Diana. "Are you thinking of singing carols now, instead of sea chanteys?"

"It's not a bad idea, folks," Mart said. "Only two hundred and some odd days till Christmas."

"No, it wasn't that, silly, but I thought that if we could use the red protest flag to cover the flashlight, it might take the place of the buoy light," answered Trixie.

"No sooner said than done," said Peter as he quickly hauled down the red pennant.

They took turns standing up and holding the flashlight as high as they could, turning it off and on at what they estimated to be six-second intervals. Just as they were beginning to worry lest the battery give out, they again heard the sound of a motor in the distance and saw a boat with a searchlight coming toward them. As it came nearer, they could hear the speed of the motor gradually being reduced. Again they stood up on the deck and yelled as loudly as they could, and soon they knew they had been sighted. A huge searchlight circled the area, and in a few minutes the boat came alongside the *Star Fire*.

"It's the Coast Guard," cried Peter when the cutter was close enough for him to see it clearly. "What a break!" He got ready to catch the line which one of the sailors was holding ready to throw to him.

"What are you doing out here at this time of night?" came an angry-sounding voice from the deck of the Coast Guard boat.

"We're not here because we want to be, sir," answered Peter. "I broke my rudder on the way back to Cobbett's Island Yacht Club, but I managed to grab on to this buoy as we drifted past it. I'm Peter Kimball, and this is my Lightning."

"So that's it." Now the voice sounded less cross. "And just how did you rig up that signal?"

"It was just a flashlight covered with red cloth," said Trixie. "Could you see it plainly?"

"Certainly could," the man answered as he jumped aboard the *Star Fire*. "I'm Captain Price of the Coast Guard," he continued as he seated himself in the stern.

After Peter had introduced his friends, the captain continued. "We've been having no end of trouble with the flashing buoys in this area. Someone apparently thinks it great sport to break the bulbs. This makes the fourth time this one has been knocked out. When I saw you tied up here, I thought I'd caught the culprit, but no such luck."

Two of the men from the Coast Guard boat had been working to replace the broken bulb, and when it started flashing again, cries of "Hurray!" and "Three cheers for the Coast Guard!" went up from the *Star Fire*.

"Personally, I'd say 'Three cheers for the *Star Fire*,'" said Captain Price, smiling at them, "and especially for Trixie here, for thinking up that emergency light."

Trixie was glad it was so dark that no one could see her face, for she knew it was flaming.

"And now, if you will be my guests, I'll give you a tow back to the club," the captain added as he stood up and prepared to board the cutter.

"I'm sorry I ever said anything mean about a stinkpot," Peter apologized. "I mean a powerboat," he added hastily. "I guess they *do* have a purpose all their own, and it's mighty lucky for us you came along when you did, sir."

"The Coast Guard is always happy to oblige," replied the captain. "You know, personally, I prefer sailboats, too, but in the service we find these—er, ahem—stinkpots more practical."

One of the crew had already released the line Peter had thrown around the buoy, and it had been made fast to the cutter. On orders from Captain Price, the big boat began to move slowly ahead, with the Lightning riding gently behind.

As they proceeded up the bay, Trixie told the captain about the yellow boat that had dashed past them earlier. "Do you think those two might have had anything to do with the broken buoy? They certainly looked as though they were up to no good."

"We've never noticed a boat of that particular description," Captain Price replied, "but we are sure that this is the work of vandals; how many, we don't know. There's a pretty rough group who hang out around Jimmy's Place, but every time we or the police go in there, it empties out as though we had the plague."

"Where's Jimmy's Place?" asked Mart.

"It's a dive near Pebble Beach on Cobbett's Island," the captain replied. "It used to be a good place to go for ice cream or a hamburger, but it was sold last year to some off-island people, and the whole character of the place has changed."

"You know," said Trixie thoughtfully, "those two in the yellow boat just might be the ones you're looking for. Would it help if *we* went down to Jimmy's and tried to pick up some information?"

"It's very good of you to suggest such a thing," said the captain, "but I'm afraid you young people wouldn't have any better luck than we. You just aren't the type to be hanging around a place like that."

"I'll bet we could get ourselves fixed up so we'd *look* the type, even if we're not," continued Trixie, not to be discouraged from her plan.

"I know we could," said Mart enthusiastically. "We know the type. They all wear the same kind of clothes, as though they were afraid to be individuals. We could dress up like them, and since none of the people on the jittery if I'm a little late getting back, even though she knows that with a sailboat you can never tell just what time you'll be in."

"I'll bet Miss Trask is frantic," chimed in Trixie. "She's been so nice about letting us do whatever we wanted since we got here, I hate to worry her."

As a matter of fact, they could see Miss Trask, Tom, and Celia at the end of the dock. Peter said, "There's Abe talking to them. He'll reassure them, all right. He's the calmest person in a crisis I've ever seen."

When finally the *Star Fire* had been made fast to her mooring, Captain Price drew alongside the dock, and the Bob-Whites scrambled ashore. As Jim and Mart helped the girls off the cutter, Peter once again thanked the captain and his crew for all their help.

"Won't you and your men come into the club and have some coffee before you go back, sir?" asked Peter.

"Thank you very much, young man. I'd like nothing better, but I don't think we'd better waste any time. I want to brief Abe on the situation before I shove off, and you know there's still work to do out there." He pointed down the bay toward the distant light which they could see still flashing its friendly warning through the darkness.

island know us, we wouldn't arouse any suspicions wl
we turn up at Jimmy's."

"Well, you certainly may try it if you want to," t
captain replied a little dubiously, "and if you get ar
information, you can always relay it through Ab
White. You know Abe, don't you?"

"One of my best friends," said Peter proudly.

The Coast Guard boat had to go slowly to keep the
Lightning on an even keel, and as they were making
their way past the Greenpoint breakwater, Trixie, who
had been standing near the pilot wheel, caught sight
of a green light and a red light in the distance. The
captain told her boats were required to carry such lights
at night. When one of the crew put the searchlight on
it, Peter saw that it was Cap in the club launch.

"They've been out looking for us," he cried. "Cap
would know, when I hadn't made port by dark, something was wrong. Good old Cap," he added warmly.

The two boats came close enough to each other
for Peter to report that all was well, and then they
headed for the club dock. As they approached land,
they saw a sizable crowd gathered on the dock, and
several flashlights were being shone across the dark
waters of the harbor. Captain Price got out a mega-
phone from the cabin and, shouting through it, assured
the crowd that all were safe.

"It looks as though our late arrival had quite a lot
of people worried," said Peter. "My mother always gets

Jimmy's Place • 10

EVERYONE WAS CROWDING around, asking questions and making sure no one had been hurt. Peter told how the rudder had been broken and how they had tied up to the buoy. He didn't say anything about the shattered light, thinking it best to keep that part of the story to himself, at least for a while. He noticed that Abe had boarded the cutter and was undoubtedly being briefed by Captain Price on that aspect of the day's adventure.

Peter and Trixie slung the sail bags over their shoulders, Mart carried the broken rudder, and Diana brought the lunch basket. As they headed for the yacht club, they saw Mrs. Kimball running toward them, an anxious look on her face.

"You're late, Mother; you've missed all the excitement," Peter called reassuringly.

"Thank heavens you're back! I waited and waited, thinking every minute you'd come in, and then I couldn't stand it another second and came down," she said breathlessly.

"We're fine, and I'll tell you all about it later," Peter said.

As they approached the clubhouse lawn, Peter saw Cap and Mart examining the rudder. Cap shook his head. "Pete, this rudder has really had it. I thought at first it might be mended temporarily, but that crack goes way up into the part that fits onto the rudder post. It would never be strong enough to be safe. I've got an extra one over at the house. I bought it from Dick after his boat was wrecked in the hurricane a couple years ago, and if you want to use it, you're more than welcome to it."

"Thanks a million, Cap," said Peter, giving his friend a thump on the back. "That would save my life. It will take at least a week to get a new one, and I'd hate not to race in the tune-ups."

"Are you still going to the clambake tomorrow?" Cap asked as they were picking up their gear, preparatory to going home.

"By Jove, I'd forgotten all about it!" Peter exclaimed. "And I promised I'd go over in the morning and help get things ready."

"I'm going over, too," rejoined Cap. "Setting up a clambake is almost as much fun as eating it. Why don't you *all* come? We'll meet at Pirate's Cove at ten. You'd all like to be initiated into the mysteries of a clambake, wouldn't you?" he asked the Bob-Whites.

"Oh, we'd love it," cried Trixie, and the others joined her in eagerly accepting the invitation.

"I don't think any of us has ever been to a real clambake. What's it like?" asked Honey.

"We won't tell you a thing about it until tomorrow," laughed Cap. "It has to be seen and eaten to be believed, doesn't it, Pete?" And with a wave of his hand, Cap was off on his bicycle.

"Jeepers, we'd better get going, too," said Trixie. "It must be awfully late."

"By my faithful chronometer, it's only nine thirty," Mart said as he looked at his wristwatch, "but it certainly seems as though we'd been out on the high seas half the night."

When they got back to The Moorings, Jim said, "I have a sneaking suspicion you didn't tell all that happened out there, Pete. Am I right?"

"You sure are!" exclaimed Trixie, and she started to tell about the broken lights and the plan they had suggested to the captain for getting further information. "And, you know, we shouldn't waste any time getting over there to Jimmy's Place," she added. "If those two in the boat get suspicious that the Coast Guard is on their trail, they may take cover for a while. How about going over tonight?"

"You're right, Trix," said Diana, "but how can we work it? I don't think we should all go, do you?"

"That's a thought, Di," Trixie said with a frown. "With Peter and all of us, there would be seven, and if we barge in there, everyone's going to notice us and wonder what's up."

"I agree," Brian said seriously. "Besides, someone from the island would be sure to spot Peter. The story of the Coast Guard rescuing us will spread like wildfire, and if those two *are* there, they'll get suspicious."

"Well, who's to go?" asked Peter. "I agree it would be taking a chance for me to go. How do you Bob-Whites decide a thing like this?"

"Oh, we don't have any set procedure. Usually someone starts out with a vague idea, and we kick it around for a while and come up with a solution. It's as simple as that."

"I suggest that our capable president and co-president be assigned to this dangerous mission," said Mart. "I know my darling sibling is secretly dying to go, and who could offer her better protection than our stalwart Jim?"

"But remember, I never saw the yellow boat," answered Jim, "and much as I'd like to go, I wouldn't be of much use, I'm afraid."

"Oh, that doesn't matter," Trixie quickly replied. "I'd know those two if I met them on a dark night in China! Come on, Jim, say you'll go."

"Okay, but there's another problem. How are we going to get there?" Jim queried. "I don't know what car we would use. Pete's would be too conspicuous."

Trixie thought for a minute, and then, snapping her fingers, she said, "I have it. We'll ask Tom to drive us all down in the station wagon. We can park a little distance from Jimmy's Place, and Jim and I can walk from there. Then, if there should be any trouble, you'll all be close enough to hear if we give the Bob-White whistle."

"That's a great idea, Sis," said Brian. "Now all we have to do is get you two dressed up, and we'll be all set."

While they quickly ate the delicious pot roast and vegetables which the cook had kept hot for them, they told Miss Trask about their plan, and she agreed to let them go if Tom would drive them. As usual, when the Bob-Whites needed him, Tom was more than willing to help.

"Now, let's see," said Trixie thoughtfully. "Jim really ought to be wearing jeans that are two sizes too small and a leather jacket, but none of us has one."

"I have a very old black jacket," volunteered Tom, who had been called in to hear about the project. "I brought it along to wear when I work on the car. You're welcome to it, if it'll be of any use."

"Wonderful, Tom; thanks a lot!" Honey replied. "It'll be just what Jim needs."

"I'll bet if Jim tries, he can wriggle into a pair of Mart's jeans," added Diana.

"Just you be careful not to stretch them," said Mart, pretending to be serious. "I'm very particular about sartorial details, you know."

"Oh, we know, Beau Brummel. You always are the mirror of fashion," said Brian. "Look at you now!" And everyone pretended to admire Mart's dirty sneakers, unpressed jeans, and badly spotted sweat shirt.

"Go on, all of you. Clothes don't make the man," Mart retorted.

"You're right; they don't," Jim remarked, "but they sometimes give a pretty good indication of what a person thinks of himself. Take those two boatmen, for example. They may be perfectly good boys, potentially, but they picture themselves as desperate characters and act accordingly."

No one noticed that Trixie had left the room with Tom. When she returned a few minutes later, everyone shrieked! She was wearing Jim's biggest sweater, which, on her, came way down below her hips. Her curly hair was hidden under a black scarf, and she was wearing a tight black skirt Celia had lent her. Her eyes, made up with eyebrow pencil and mascara, looked completely unnatural.

"Trixie Belden, where did you get that rig?" yelled Jim, not knowing at first whether to be annoyed or amused by her outlandish getup.

"Celia helped me," giggled Trixie. "It seems that when she and Tom go out for an evening, she sometimes puts on a bit of eye makeup. She helped me put on not just a bit but scads of the stuff!" Trixie gingerly wiped the corner of one eye with her little finger. "And the skirt is part of the uniform she wears when she serves dinner."

Tom came back at this moment with the jacket, and, seeing Trixie, he burst out laughing. "I'd never believe it, Trixie; you should be an actress."

"She'll end up being the world's greatest female sleuth, or I miss my guess," said Brian.

"She's really one already," added Jim admiringly. "Come on, away to work, Sherlock Holmes. You all get into the car, and I'll dash up and change into Mart's jeans," he said as he ran up the stairs, pulling on Tom's jacket as he went.

Everyone was laughing and joking as they piled into the station wagon and headed for Pebble Beach. Tom said he knew where it was, because he and Celia had gone there swimming on their day off. He parked the car in a dark spot off the road, some distance from the roadhouse. A blue neon sign proclaimed to the world that this was, indeed, Jimmy's Place. Cars were parked in front of the brightly lighted building, and they could hear the blare of the jukebox and the raucous laughter of what apparently was a good-sized crowd.

Jim and Trixie got out of the station wagon and

headed down the road. "Jeepers, Jim," she said nervously, "I don't know if this was such a brilliant idea or not. I've never been in a place like this in my life, and I—"

Jim took firm hold of her hand and said, "Don't worry, Trix; I'll bet there's more noise than danger in there. We'll look in the window first, and then we'll plan our attack."

Trixie felt ashamed of her momentary panic and was glad that none of the others had heard her remark, but she knew that Jim understood how she felt. She said in a low voice, "Gee, Jim, I'm awfully glad it was you they picked to come tonight. Thanks for calming me down." For an answer, Jim gave her hand a squeeze.

They strolled up to the front of Jimmy's Place and tried to look as casual as possible. They saw a couple come out and start up the road in the opposite direction. Through the window, they could make out a crowd around a jukebox. Others were leaning against the bar in the rear or sitting in the high-backed booths that occupied one side of the smoke-filled room.

"Come on, Trix," said Jim, pulling her toward the door. "Chin up."

"Hey, not so fast," Trixie whispered as she pressed her face closer to the window. "See that bunch of boys over there in the first booth? I've got a hunch that if there's dirty work going on around here, they'd know about it. They're the same type as those characters in the motorboat. In fact, they may be the same ones."

"Okay, Trixie," Jim answered. "Let's go on in and head for that empty booth right behind them, before anyone beats us to it. We won't be conspicuous there, and we can at least get the lay of the land."

They took a last look down the road to the car to reassure themselves, then pushed their way inside. They sat down opposite each other in the booth. Jim realized they would have to order something if they didn't want to attract attention, although neither of them relished the idea of eating here. He asked for a ham sandwich and a Coke for each of them.

While they were waiting for their order, they glanced around to see if any of the crowd were the ones they were looking for and realized that practically any of the boys in the place might be the ones Trixie had seen in the yellow speedboat. She ruefully conceded that she didn't have as clear a picture as she had at first thought.

"Why do I always act so impulsively?" she moaned. "I was sure I'd know those two, and now I couldn't be more puzzled. It must be awful when you have to try to identify someone in a police lineup. I'll bet there are loads of mistakes made and a lot of people are accused of things they never did."

"Don't worry about that now, Trix. We may not find out anything tonight, but I'm sure that eventually they'll be caught. You can't get by with that kind of stuff for very long, you know," Jim reassured her.

They were silent for a while, taking occasional tiny bites from the unpalatable sandwiches and listening to the flow of talk around them. All of a sudden Trixie put her finger to her lips and motioned over her shoulder at the booth behind her. She put her head close to the back of the booth, listening intently. Jim wasn't able to hear anything except the general din around him, so he just sat perfectly still. Finally Trixie leaned over the table and whispered, "Let's get out of here, Jim. Quick!"

He put the money for the food on the table, and they left. They raced back to the car.

"Did you find them?" asked Brian, impatient for news, as they all were.

"No," gasped Trixie, trying to get her breath, "but I have some really good leads—at least, I *think* I have," she declared, remembering this time to be a little more cautious.

"Hurry up and tell us," said Jim. "Even *I* don't know what Trixie found out in there."

"Well, before we went in I looked through the window and spotted some boys who looked kind of suspicious. So we went in and sat in the booth right back of them," Trixie began.

"Oh, step on it, Trix. Skip the details and tell us what you found out," Mart urged her impatiently.

"Anyway, I caught the words 'flashing buoy,' so I pressed my ear right up against the back of the booth and heard most of the conversation. One of them was boasting that some guy in Greenpoint had asked him to go out and shoot out the buoy lights. He said it was Slim something-or-other who had thought up that little caper. It sounded like a foreign name. I couldn't hear it clearly. Anyway, it seems Slim was sore about being turned down by the Coast Guard and swore he was going to keep them hopping."

"Good work, Trix. At least you got part of his name and where he's from. Were you scared?" asked Honey.

Trixie looked at Jim and conceded that she was glad he had been with her. "That's quite a joint!" she said. "But now we should get this information to Abe, don't you think?"

"We can telephone him as soon as we get back," Brian suggested. "I hope he doesn't think this is another wild-goose chase."

"You can bet he won't. Not after what Captain Price must have told him tonight!" Trixie exclaimed.

It was later than usual by the time they all got to bed, and everyone was glad of being able to sleep a little later the next morning. Once the excitement let up, they realized they were more tired than they had thought.

Trixie tossed and turned in her bed, unable to go to sleep, with visions of Jimmy's Place, the chart, the coming clambake, and the open sea going round and round in her head.

Diana, realizing how restless Trixie was, got out
of bed and very quietly, so as not to disturb Honey,
went into the bathroom, returning with a washcloth
which she had wrung out of cold water. She sat on
the edge of Trixie's bed and put the folded cloth on her
forehead, patting her arm gently until she felt the
tension ease. Before long, Trixie yawned sleepily and
mumbled, "Thanks, Di. Good night." It was only a few
minutes, then, before they were both asleep.

The Captain's Tales • 11

THE BOB-WHITES were just finishing breakfast the next morning when they heard the familiar *beep-beep* of the Icebox. Honey ran out to tell Peter they would be ready in a minute. "We always have to wait for Mart to finish the last bite of toast or pancake or whatever we're having," she said. "I think his legs are hollow."

The others came out almost immediately, and Peter smiled when he saw Mart with a half-eaten bun in his hand. "I bet we'll fill you up tonight, Mart Belden," he said as they were getting into the car. "You've never seen so much food in your life as they have at one of these clambakes."

"Who's giving it?" Trixie asked as they were driving off.

"It's the yacht club's opening party," Peter answered. "Some of us pitch in and help set it up, but it's really

supervised by old Captain Clark. He's the island clambake expert. He's a real character."

Pirate's Cove was on the other side of the island from
The Moorings. It was approached by a dirt road that
twisted and turned through woods of scrub oak, locust,
and wild cherry trees. Peter told them the whole area
was a game sanctuary, and as he drove slowly along,
they saw a doe looking at them warily from the trees.
Jim, who was a great nature lover, pointed out a fawn,
whose dappled baby coat made it almost invisible
among the leaves of the underbrush. A cock pheasant
sauntered jauntily across the road in front of the car,
as if to show off his brilliant plumage and beautiful long
tail. A covey of quail rattled up into the air from their
hiding place in the leaves.

"I guess they don't recognize their bobwhite cousins,"
Brian remarked, but when Peter stopped the car and
Jim imitated the little crooning noise the birds make
when feeding, he was able to lure them back into
view.

"What a wonderful place this would be for my
camp!" exclaimed Jim, whose fondest dream was to
establish a year-round outdoor school for children who,
like himself, had been orphaned.

Pirate's Cove was a quiet little bay, surrounded by
a broad stretch of sand. Peter said it got its name from
the legend that a pirate had once been forced to take
refuge there and might have buried his treasure on

shore. "Every island I've ever heard of has its favorite pirate," he added with a laugh, "so Cobbett's is not to be outdone; but, so far, no one has found a thing except Indian arrowheads and stone utensils."

"Even Sleepyside has a legend about Captain Kidd," Trixie said. "He must have been quite a traveler!"

As they piled out of the car, they saw a huge fire already burning in a shallow pit down on the beach. An old man was adding pieces of driftwood, with the help of Cap and some other boys.

"Come on, slowpokes!" yelled Cap as he came up to meet them. "Help us bring some big rocks. The fire's almost ready for them."

"Rocks on a fire?" Trixie queried, her brows furrowed in bewilderment.

"It does sound crazy," said Peter, "but the idea is to get the rocks as hot as possible and then cover them with wet seaweed."

"That would make steam, I gather, but where does the food fit into the picture?" asked Brian.

"Are you embarking on a scientific investigation of this mysterious process, or are you just making sure you won't have to eat algae for supper?" quipped Mart.

"I'm merely taking careful note of the procedure for future reference, dear brother. Here, grab a rock!" Brian tossed a big stone to Mart, who, pretending to be knocked down as he caught it, rolled over and over in the sand.

Peter, introducing them to Captain Clark, said, "Our island's most eminent seafarer. Captain Clark's been sailing since he was a boy of—how old, Captain?"

"I was twelve when I first went to sea, just sixty years ago, come July," Captain Clark answered in a booming voice.

He was a huge man with thick hair, which was almost white, and a heavy beard. Trixie thought, as she looked at him, that he would make a perfect Santa Claus if he were dressed for the part. Instead, he was wearing faded blue denim pants, held up by an intricately woven rope belt, and a red and white striped shirt that accentuated the breadth of his shoulders and the girth of his chest. His arms were tattooed, from elbows to wrists, with assorted mermaids, ships, and anchors. Very bright blue eyes shone out from under his shaggy brows, and in a stentorian voice he was barking orders to "set to lively and heave up the rocks, else we'll have no clambake tonight."

Once the stones on the fire were hot, they were covered with seaweed. Then Captain Clark led them all up to his truck, which was parked in the shade near the edge of the woods. He pulled back a canvas that covered a great variety of baskets. Some contained clams; some, ears of corn still in their husks; and in still others there were plump chickens wrapped in cheese-cloth. There were lobsters; and there was a basket of potatoes, each of which had been wrapped in aluminum foil. Everything was carried to the fire and laid on top of the seaweed. When the captain had checked to be sure each item was in its proper place, an enormous tarpaulin was carefully spread over the whole pile and weighted down with sand that the boys shoveled on top of it.

"Now, we'll let this steam all day, and tonight—" Words failed the captain as he thought of the succulent feast, and so he merely kissed the fingers of his right hand and looked to the heavens, in an elaborate gesture of anticipation.

Everyone had been so busy there had been little time for talk, but now that the work was done, they went down to the edge of the beach to scoop up water onto their hot faces and to dip their tired feet. After they had cooled off, they sat down in the shade of the trees, and Cap called to the captain, who was still fussing around the clambake to be sure everything was in the proper order, to tell them a story.

"Why, son, you've heard just about every yarn in my book," Captain Clark replied. "I'd be hard put to it to find another."

"You always say that, Captain Clark, but I have yet to see the time when you couldn't come up with a fine tale," Cap said as the old man came over to join them.

The captain sat down in their midst, and, after pulling on his pipe for several minutes while he gazed out to sea, he asked, "Did I ever tell you about the *Eastern Belle?*" He took another draw on his pipe as he waited for a reaction.

There were cries of "No. Please tell us. Go on, Captain," from everyone.

Shifting his pipe to the other side of his mouth, Captain Clark settled back against the trunk of a tree and began.

"Back when I was a lad, I was asked by old Mr. Atwood to sail the *Eastern Belle* down to the Bahamas. She had been built right here on the island years before and was used in the whaling trade all up and down the east coast in the days when people used sperm oil in their lamps. But after kerosene came in, the whalers didn't go out anymore, or if they did, it was only for the small amount of sperm oil that was needed for special purposes. So the *Eastern Belle* was just sitting out her time in port. She was a beautiful boat, stoutly built, and on her bow was a figurehead of a young woman dressed in white, with golden hair flowing over her shoulders and her arms crossed in front of her.

"Well, one day Mr. Atwood came to the shipyard where the *Belle* had been put up, and he fell in love with her. He had more money than he knew what to do with. Seems his father had made it mining, so he could indulge himself with what he liked better than anything else on earth—boats. He had her put into shape, got new sails, and had the living quarters made comfortable. It was then I got a chance to take her south.

"I didn't have any trouble getting a crew, for the *Belle* was known as a good ship, and the trip promised to be a pleasant one. So one fine morning in May, we set out, rounding Montauk Point at dawn. I can see her now, with her canvas drawing sweetly in the strong breeze that took us at a fine clip for several days. Then we hit the doldrums, where the equatorial calms had us sitting day after day in the hot sun, without enough breeze to put out a match. Well, sir, tempers began to get a mite edgy, but just when we were all secretly beginning to regret not having an engine in the ship, the winds came up again as suddenly as they had failed, and we were away, heading for one of the little-known Bahama Islands, where we planned to anchor.

"After a couple of fine days' sailing, late one afternoon we heard the cry 'Land ho' from our lookout and knew that we were not far from our destination. We made for a small cove, not much bigger than this one here, that we knew was deep enough to enter. As we got up close enough to make out the trees on shore, the lookout called again. He'd seen people on the beach, running up and down and waving their hands. Now, we didn't think this particular island was inhabited, and there wasn't a sign of another boat around, so we were all mighty curious to know who these folks were.

"It didn't take long to launch a dory and row in. I went and took a couple of men to man the oars, and it was lucky we arrived just when we did. Those people we'd seen through the telescope were from a small fishing boat that had shipped out from Florida. The boat had caught fire and had been completely destroyed. Six of the crew had managed to swim to the island, where they'd been living on fish and fruit for almost two weeks. Ours was the first ship they'd seen, and as we came ashore, their joy was overwhelming, tears mingling with laughter. After we had taken them on board the *Eastern Belle*, we gave them clean clothes and plenty to eat. The next day we took all of them back to their home port. You should have seen how happy they were!

"Now, off with you, and let me have my nap." The old man chuckled as he knocked the ashes out of his pipe, clasped his hands over his stomach, and closed his eyes.

"That means we won't get any more yarns," Cap said as they prepared to leave, "but maybe tonight he'll tell us another one."

"See you later, then," Peter said, "and don't forget to bring your accordion. It wouldn't be a clambake without that."

Toward the end of the afternoon, after a swim and a couple of hours on the beach, they gathered at Pirate's Cove again. There was a goodly crowd already there, and more people were arriving every moment. Captain Clark and some of the other men were getting ready to remove the tarpaulin. Much of the sand had been shoveled off, but great care had to be taken that none of what remained got into the food. The delicious aroma of the clambake was the only invitation anyone needed to start eating. Plates were piled high, first with steamed clams and lobsters slathered with melted butter from the bowls laid out on tables here and there around the pit. Chicken and vegetables would come later.

Mart was in seventh heaven. Peter's prediction was quickly being proved right, and he was being filled up at a great rate!

"Don't forget there's still chicken, corn, and potatoes," warned Peter as Mart went up to get a third helping of clams.

"Is that a warning or a suggestion?" Mart asked, laughing.

"I don't want you to miss the best part," Peter answered him, "but I guess you'll manage without any cues from me."

The other Bob-Whites were managing about as well as Mart. "Have you ever tasted such delicious food?" Trixie exclaimed. "I'm about ready to burst, but I'm going to have one more ear of corn if it kills me!"

Honey and Di, who had already eaten their fill, started out with Peter and Brian for a walk down the

beach. "We'll come along, too, in a few minutes," Trixie
called after them, "if we can manage to get on our feet."

When everyone had finished eating, more driftwood
was put on the coals in the pit, and soon a cheery fire
encouraged the guests to sing. A circle was formed,
and Cap brought out his accordion and played all the
old favorite songs. Trixie, who, during the stroll on the
beach, had been thinking about Captain Clark and his
yarns, managed to get a seat next to him and, when a
lull came in the songfest, said, "What about the menhaden boats, Captain Clark? Did you ever go out on
them?"

"Yes, young lady. The last time I sailed on a trans-
atlantic boat, I had an experience that made me decide
never to go across the ocean again, but that's another
story," he mused, his eyes looking dreamily into the
fire. "But I couldn't seem to find anything on land that
I fancied, not after so many years at sea, so I started
going out on the bunker boats. It wasn't a hard life. I
knew the waters hereabouts like the palm of my hand,
and the crew did all the hard work, so I continued to
go out for several years." He paused and then rather
abruptly said, "How'd you happen to ask about the
bunker boats, young lady?"

Trixie told him she was staying at The Moorings,
and that she could see the boats from her window
there and had found herself fascinated by them.

"You're in the old Condon place, then," the Captain

continued, eyeing her quizzically. "Well, that reminds me of something that happened—let me see, it must have been eighteen or twenty years ago. It was in the winter. We'd started out in good weather, and the fish were running out beyond Montauk. We'd worked two or three days, and the holds were just about filled with fish, when it began to sleet and snow. The winds blew harder and harder, and I soon saw we were in for a real blow. I gave orders to batten down the hatches and prepared to ride it out, not thinking it would last very long. But it stormed like fury all day and all night. The seas got higher and higher, and, although I tried to make some headway, I couldn't keep her on course. I began to think we'd end up on the rocks at the end of the point. That was before the bunker boats had radios. I don't suppose we could see more than twenty feet in front of us; the snow and sleet were that thick. All we could do was blow our foghorn to warn any other ship that might be near us. We were pretty helpless.

"Suddenly, out of nowhere, we saw it—another bunker boat coming toward us out of the night. As the lookout yelled, 'Ship ahoy,' I instinctively spun the pilot wheel around to ward off the blow, but it was too late. Even though the other boat tried to move off in the other direction, we couldn't avoid the collision. We rammed into her side amidships, a little above the waterline but right where the engine room was. It was a good thing I could reverse our engines and pull off, because fire broke out almost immediately. I've never seen anything spread so fast. The crew tried to fight it at first, but the captain soon saw it was hopeless and gave orders for his men to abandon ship.

"I worked our boat around to their windward side. There was enough breeze blowing to keep the heat and smoke from that part of the ship, and the men jumped across to our deck. Everyone was relieved when the captain himself came across, for we thought that meant all the crew had been saved. But just then our lookout called down that he could see another man on the fore-deck, and it looked as though he had been hurt.

"By this time the ship was an inferno, and I didn't think we'd have time to try to rescue another without being set afire ourselves, but before I'd even had time to make up my mind, one of our men had jumped across to the other deck and was running forward to try to save the injured man. We could see him lift him up, sling him over his shoulder, and carry him to the rail, where he heaved him over to our boat. Then Ed—that was his name—jumped over himself. That is, he started to jump, but he missed his footing and fell between the boats, into the sea."

The captain stopped here, and Trixie knew he was having a hard time trying to continue. This was not just another sea story. This was a tragedy in which he had been personally involved. Trixie hoped he would continue, but she resolved not to ask a single question which might trouble this old man who looked so strong but who, she now knew, was most tenderhearted.

"So the sea took its toll again," he finally continued. "We searched the water all that night and the next day, even when we knew it was hopeless. You may wonder what all this has to do with the old Condon place," he continued, looking questioningly at Trixie. "Well, I'll tell you. Mr. Condon had always been fond of Ed and advised him and such, and when he heard that Ed was gone, the shock killed him. Yes, two days after we got back to port, Mr. Condon, too, was gone, and no one left to live in his big house. He willed it to a distant niece out in California, and she's rented it out ever since. Well, that's it, young lady. So when you look over the harbor to the bunker boats, just think of a young man who didn't think twice about giving his life for someone he didn't even know. He was a hero, that Ed."

Before Trixie had time to do more than thank him for telling her the story, the captain had gone away to see about cleaning up the remains of the clambake. Trixie turned to Jim, who had been sitting next to her, and said, "So now we know. Ed *was* a real person."

The Mysterious Stranger · 12

CAN YOU IMAGINE? The garden party is this afternoon!" exclaimed Trixie. "I don't see how we'll ever get ready in time!"

"I simply have to wash my hair. It's full of sand from last night," said Honey as she brushed it vigorously, "and it must smell like burning brush from all that smoke."

"Do you think the dresses we brought will be all right?" Di asked.

"I guess they'll have to be," Honey answered. "Now that Mrs. Kimball has asked us to help, I wish we had something special to wear so we wouldn't look like guests."

"Yes," mused Trixie, "something like the Spanish costumes we wore in the winter carnival, only different, if you know what I mean."

"Well, I can't think of anything we could dream up on the spur of the moment, can you?" asked Di.

"No," answered Trixie slowly, "not unless—"

"Not unless what, Trix? Something tells me you have one of your inspirations. Let's have it," cried Diana.

"Well, I was just thinking. Remember all those trunks in the attic at Peter's house? Maybe there are some old-fashioned clothes up there that we could dress up in. People used to keep stuff like that, you know."

"That's an absolutely brilliant idea, Trix," exclaimed Honey. "Let's go down and call Peter and see if his mother minds if we look through them. You know, he said the other day that he always meant to explore up there but never had the time."

"Even if we don't find any dresses, it'll be fun to see what's in the trunks," added Di as they went to phone.

"But what about the gazebo?" Honey asked, stopping abruptly halfway down the stairs. "There's still a terrific amount of work to do on it before the party."

"Oh, jeepers, I forgot all about that," said Trixie dismally, sitting down on the bottom stair with her chin in her hands. "But I know what," she said, her face almost immediately brightening. "We'll let the boys take care of that little problem. You know how manly they acted about not wanting us to use the chain saw? Well, now we'll flatter them into thinking they're the only ones who could possibly know enough about carpentry to do the job.".

"Good idea, if it works," answered Honey, somewhat dubiously. "Let's not tell them anything about what we're going to do, and after they get to work, we can ask Mrs. Kimball if she'll let us try our plan."

"Quiet, here come our unsuspecting victims now," said Trixie as she got up and sauntered into the dining room.

"What's up?" asked Jim as he and the others came in. "You look like three cats that have just swallowed three fat canaries."

"Why, nothing's up," answered Trixie, her eyes innocently wide. "We were just trying to figure out what to do with ourselves this morning while you boys are fixing that broken board and the pillar in the gazebo."

"You're going to *help* us. That's what you're going to do," said Mart. "What else?"

"We'd *love* to. You *know* we would, but that's a job for experts, and we'd just be in the way," Di commented, looking helplessly feminine.

"Yes, you know how clumsy girls are with tools," Honey went on, "so it would be much better if we left the whole thing to you. The job will get done quicker that way."

"Okay," said Jim, looking quizzically at Trixie. "It's quite obvious the girls have something up their sleeves, and we might as well try to get water out of a rock as to get secret plans from any of these three."

"Trixie probably lured them into some private sleuthing," said Brian. "Wait till they come running back to us for help."

"Are you going over to Peter's with us, or do your clandestine activities lead you to more distant fields?" inquired Mart.

"If you must know, dear brother, we're going over to see if we can help Mrs. Kimball get things ready," answered Trixie with a toss of her head. "It really wouldn't be fair not to help, after all Peter has done for us."

"So any more work on the chart will have to wait until after the party," Jim commented.

When they arrived at the Oldest House, Mrs. Kimball greeted them warmly and said Peter was out in the toolshed getting ready to finish the repairs on the gazebo.

"And I'm polishing extra spoons and washing more china, just in case we have an overflow crowd," she added.

"We'd better step on it, or Peter'll think we've left him in the lurch," Jim said as he headed out the door.

"See you squaws later," Mart called out to the girls, "and don't take any wooden wampum!"

Trixie threw him a withering glance and then, turning to Mrs. Kimball, asked, "Isn't there something we could do to help you get ready?"

"That's sweet of you to ask, but my committee is coming any minute now, and I think we have things

pretty well under control, especially since you're going
to help out as hostesses," she answered. "Thank goodness the weather's cooperating, too."

"If you're sure we can't help right now, would you
mind if we—" Trixie hesitated and felt the color rising
in her cheeks.

"What, Trixie?" Mrs. Kimball replied. "I'm sure anything you have in mind is all right with me. Out with it!"

Her gay laugh reassured Trixie that she wasn't being
forward, so she went on, "We thought that maybe up in
your attic we might find some old-fashioned dresses we
could wear this afternoon."

"What a charming idea!" exclaimed Mrs. Kimball.
"I haven't the slightest idea what's up there, but you
most certainly may look. You can go right up the back
stairs here from the kitchen."

The girls could hardly wait to start their search.
After thanking Mrs. Kimball, they dashed up the two
flights of stairs to the attic.

"Which one shall we try first?" asked Honey, looking around at the many boxes and trunks lined up
under the eaves.

"This one looks interesting," said Trixie, going over
to an old brassbound trunk.

As she lifted the cover, the faint odor of sandalwood
mingled with the special scent of the old room, where,
long ago, various herbs had been hung to dry. "Oh, this
smells just like the Chinese box Miss Rachel gave me,"

sighed Trixie as she thought of the Bob-Whites' adventure in the marshlands.

In the top of the trunk was a tray that held an assortment of fans, tortoiseshell combs, and bits of lace and ribbons. "Hurry and look underneath!" cried Di as Honey and Trixie lifted the tray out of the trunk and put it carefully down on the floor.

Trixie's hunch had been right. There were layers of old dresses, some of soft wool, others of silk. Most of them were so old that the fabric had begun to split. "Here's one that looks strong enough to wear," said Honey, carefully unfolding a moss-green skirt. "I wonder if there's a top to go with it."

"Here it is, under this shawl," cried Trixie excitedly. "Try it on, Honey. The color is simply wonderful for you!"

Honey hurriedly stepped into the full skirt, which came to her ankles. The top fitted perfectly, too. She twirled around the attic, making the skirt billow out about her.

"Oh, it's just perfect, Honey," said Di. "I hope Trix and I have as good luck. Come on, let's keep looking."

They reached the bottom of the trunk, however, without finding anything that seemed in good enough condition to wear, so they quickly moved on to the next one, which, to their great disappointment, held nothing but old books and papers.

"They're probably fascinating, but they're not what

we're after right now. Well, here goes the third one," said Trixie as she started to lift the cover. "Keep your fingers crossed."

Luck was with them, for this trunk, like the first, was filled with dresses. "There must have been an awful lot of women in this family," Di said as she lifted out a lovely ashes-of-roses dress. "This may fit, but the waist looks pretty snug. I'll have to hold my breath and not eat any cookies, or I'll burst a seam!"

"*You* burst a seam! What about me?" cried Trixie. "I know I couldn't get into any of these. I'm sure I've gained five pounds since I came down here."

"Don't be silly," answered Honey. "Your figure's perfect, and your waist is inches smaller than it was last summer."

Di, who had been rummaging through the trunk as the other two were talking, pulled out a challis dress that was just the color of a ripe pumpkin.

"How perfectly darling!" cried Honey. "Trix, this just *has* to fit you. Hurry and try it on."

Trixie lost no time getting into the bright little dress. This one, unlike the others, buttoned down the back, so she asked Honey to help her.

"Come on over to the window so I can see what I'm doing," Honey said. "These little loops are so tiny, I'm having trouble." She led Trixie over to one of the attic windows which looked over the backyard. While Honey struggled with the buttons, Trixie glanced outside. She suddenly started to yell but caught herself and clapped one hand over her mouth. With the other she pointed in the direction of the toolshed.

Di hurried over just in time to see what had upset Trixie. All three saw someone running into the woods, and that someone was wearing a black jacket!

"I'll bet it's one of those two in the yellow boat!" Trixie cried. "Come on. Let's get him!"

They started to run out but realized all too soon that they were hopelessly encumbered by their long skirts. "It's no use," Trixie moaned. "He'll be miles away by the time we even get downstairs with these things on, and the boys are too far away to hear us, even if we did whistle for them. Besides," she added, "we'd never hear the last of it if we had to ask them for help at this point."

"What in the world do you suppose he was doing around here?" asked Di, still peering out of the window.

"I can't imagine, but I have a sneaking suspicion he's been here before, and it could be he's one of the two who spent the night in the loft," Trixie answered.

"What do you suppose happened to the other one?" Honey asked. "Of course, there could have been two running into the woods, and we just saw one of them."

"Help me out of this thing," Trixie cried, trying to wriggle out of her dress. "You know, if I hadn't had that brilliant idea about dressing up, we might have been able to catch him or at least trail him. I always did say skirts were an awful nuisance."

"Oh, don't blame yourself, Trixie," Honey consoled her. "He probably thinks no one saw him, so he may come back. After all, we don't *know* he was up to anything."

"Maybe you're right," Trixie conceded, "and I suppose we ought to tell the boys, so they'll be on the lookout, too, but let's not say anything about it to Peter's mother. As Honey says, we don't *know* he was doing anything wrong, and it might upset her, with the party on her mind and Mr. Kimball away and all."

After they had dressed in their own clothes, the girls carefully repacked the things they were not going to use and closed the trunks. As they were about to go downstairs, Mrs. Kimball called to ask if they had had any luck.

"We're on our way down now," Trixie answered. "We'll show you."

Mrs. Kimball was delighted when she saw what they had found. At her suggestion, they left the dresses in the guest room to be ironed, and then they hurried toward the gazebo, where they could hear the boys hammering away.

"It looks absolutely super!" Trixie called out as they approached.

"Look, they've even fixed the weather vane," cried Di, pointing to the little ship, which was moving in the light breeze.

"And the floor is as good as new," Honey added as she jumped up and down to test it.

"Now, if you're about finished, we have news for you," said Trixie as she sat down on one of the benches. "Guess what."

"Trixie's found the mon-ey! Trixie's found the money!" chanted Mart, clapping his hands.

"Oh, stop acting like an idiot!" Trixie said fiercely. "I'm serious. Someone's been lurking around here this morning, and we saw him take off through the woods back of the toolshed just a few minutes ago, and he was wearing—"

"A black jacket, I'll bet," said Brian.

"Right, but he was too far away for us to tell what he looked like. All we could see was his back. But he was sort of tall."

"Why didn't you follow him, Trix? I never knew you to pass up a chance to follow a hot lead before," quipped Mart with a broad grin.

"We were up in the attic when we saw him, that's why," Honey answered. "So don't blame Trixie, Mart Belden. You know she would have trailed him if she could."

"In the attic!" cried Brian. "For pete's sake, what were you doing up there?"

"Oh, I had an idea that if we wore old-fashioned costumes this afternoon, it might be kind of an added attraction," Trixie explained, "and Mrs. Kimball let us look up there in those old trunks."

"Did you have any luck, or did the mysterious stranger interrupt you?" Mart persisted.

"You'll just have to wait and see," Honey replied.

"Okay, but you're not the only ones with a secret," Jim said, "so you'll have to 'wait and see,' too."

The girls tried unsuccessfully to wheedle Jim into telling them what he meant, but he only said, " 'What's sauce for the goose is sauce for the gander.' Now we'd better get back to the house and let them know that the gazebo is fixed."

"We'll go and tell Mrs. Kimball while you take the tools back," volunteered Trixie, "and then I want to have a look around the shed and see if there are any signs of anyone's fooling around out there."

The girls ran back to the house and then hurried to the shed, arriving there just as Jim was hanging up the last of the tools.

"I can't see that anything is missing," said Peter, giving a cursory glance around the room, "but maybe your eagle eyes will find some clues."

Trixie went upstairs but returned almost immediately. "Everything's just the way we left it up there," she announced. "Now, let's see. No cigarette butts down here, no footprints, no— Hey, wait a minute!" she cried as her eyes swept around the walls. "No calendar! Pete, did you take it into the house?"

"By Jove, I didn't. After I made the copy of the

map, I left it right here on the workbench, and I'm pretty sure it was here this morning," he answered as he looked under the bench and around the room.

"Could it have blown away?" asked Di, looking outside the door.

"Not a chance. The calendar had a heavy metal binder, and there hasn't been more than a light breeze blowing all day," Peter replied thoughtfully, scratching his head in puzzlement.

"No, someone took it!" Trixie said fiercely. "And I'm afraid our secret is out of the bag. If we're being spied on, we'll all have to make a special effort to act as though nothing has happened. And we'll have to keep our eyes and ears open."

Teacups and Sailboats · 13

DURING LUNCH Trixie seemed unusually quiet, despite Jim's efforts to draw her into the conversation. "What's on your mind, Trix?" he asked as she continued to toy with her food.

"Oh, I don't know. It all seems so kind of hopeless," she answered. "Honey and I had better think twice about being detectives, if we can't do any better than this."

"Don't be discouraged," Honey reassured her. "We've often lost the trail before, but something always turns up to steer us back on the right road."

"You know you have the full cooperation of all the B.W.G.'s, plus Peter, and our *esprit de corps* has never been higher," added Mart earnestly, seeming to realize that this was no time to tease his sister.

"Thanks, Mart," Trixie answered warmly. "You're all

truly wonderful, honest you are."

"Let's not think about it right now," Diana suggested, feeling that time was the only thing that could ease the situation.

"You're right, Di. We'll enjoy the party and just hope for the best," Honey agreed.

"I intend to have a good time, too, but I'm still going to keep *thinking*, for goodness' sake!" Trixie impatiently pushed her chair away from the table and started upstairs. Honey and Di followed, concerned about Trixie's black mood.

"She'll snap out of it," Honey whispered to Di. "I've never known her to be glum very long."

After they had bathed and dressed, they combed their hair and, slipping into their black flats, hurried over to the Oldest House to change into their costumes. The boys had gone on ahead to help carry tables and chairs out to the garden. Everyone was in a bustle of excitement when the girls arrived.

"My committee says practically everyone on the island is coming," Mrs. Kimball said after greeting them. "Peter says the boys are going to help him park the cars down in the lower field. Trixie, will you sit out on the porch and sell the tickets for us?"

"Anything you say, Mrs. Kimball," said Trixie cheerfully, the old sparkle coming back into her eyes. Honey and Di exchanged winks.

"Di and Honey, I'd like you to direct the guests out

to our gazebo for tea, and tell them to feel free to look through the gardens," Mrs. Kimball continued. "The roses are at their best right now. By the way, have you all seen the gazebo since we set up the tea things? It turned out better than I imagined it could!"

"Let's go take a look, and then we'd better get into our dresses before we get caught by an early arrival," suggested Honey.

"Jeepers!" exclaimed Trixie as they approached the gazebo. "It doesn't look like the same place at all. How perfectly darling!"

"The committee must have worked awfully hard to get it decorated in such a short time. Look at the festoons of greens around the columns. You'd never know the paint was peeling," said Honey.

"What's that on the table?" asked Di as she went inside.

"That must be what the boys meant when they said they had a surprise," said Trixie.

On the table, in front of a beautiful arrangement of flowers, was a model of a colonial building. A sign on it read: MODEL OF THE PROPOSED COBBETT'S ISLAND PUBLIC LIBRARY. Just then Mrs. Kimball came in, carrying a tray of silver, and explained that Peter had started the model in school but had not had time to complete it. With the help of Jim and the others, it had been finished this morning.

"I thought they were taking a long time to fix a

couple of boards and a broken pillar," Trixie said, "but they certainly kept this a deep, dark secret."

"It took a bit of doing, but they managed to smuggle it out of Peter's room without you girls suspecting a thing," Mrs. Kimball laughed.

It didn't take the girls long to dress, and they were ready on the porch as the first guests walked up from the parking lot. More and more people followed, and Trixie had to work fast to see that everyone had a ticket and the proper change. Honey and Di, after escorting a party to the gazebo, would run back to the house, as fast as their skirts would permit, to greet another group. The line seemed endless. Mrs. Kimball saw that extra cookies and cakes were taken out as supplies became depleted. She seemed able to be in several places at once, chatting with guests and seeing that everything was going smoothly.

By five o'clock the last guest had departed, the committee had finished cleaning up, and Mrs. Kimball, looking tired but happy, joined the Bob-Whites and Peter on the porch. Jim, noticing that Trixie was counting the money, asked, "What's the take, Trix? By the number of cars we handled this afternoon, we must have made a fortune."

"Thirteen, fourteen, fifteen," Trixie counted out loud. "Two hundred and fifteen dollars!" she exclaimed. "Wow!"

"Wow, indeed," Mrs. Kimball laughingly repeated.

"And that's all free and clear, because the food was do-
nated. How can I ever thank all of you Bob-Whites
for your help?"

" 'He is well paid who is well satisfied,' as Mr. Shake-
speare once put it," Jim replied.

"We certainly don't need any thanks," Trixie added.
"Jim's right. The whole thing has really been fun."

"Besides the money we made, the party helped pub-
licize the Library Fund," Mrs. Kimball went on. "Several people told me they hadn't been especially interested in the building until they saw the model. Now
they intend to make a substantial donation. Now, tell
me, what have you planned for tomorrow? You deserve
a day of rest after the way you've worked."

Trixie, not wanting to divulge their plan of further
work on the chart, told her they'd probably spend the
day on the beach or looking around the island.

"And we must go and call on El. We've neglected him
since his accident," Jim added.

The Bob-Whites had been so busy at the tea that
even Mart hadn't found time to eat any of the delicious cakes or cookies, so by dinner time they were all
starved. Since Miss Trask hadn't known what time
they would be home from the party, she had suggested
that the cook prepare a cold supper for them. A large
bowl of potato salad, assorted sliced meats, coleslaw,
and dessert were waiting for them on the buffet.

"Let's take trays out on the porch," suggested Honey, when they had all served themselves. "It'll soon be time for the sunset, and it should be another beauty."

As they ate, they watched the sky in the west change from a purple blue to rose, orange, and red as the sun sank behind the yacht club across the bay. They discussed the party at length and found that, although they all had been on the lookout for strange visitors, no one had seen anything suspicious.

Just as they were finishing, they saw Peter loping down the road toward The Moorings. "Hi, neighbors. Long time no see," he called out as he came up the porch steps, two at a time.

"No, it's been ages," Trixie answered. "All of two hours!"

"What brings you to the hallowed halls of Wheeler?" Mart asked as he passed the last remaining piece of orange cake to Peter.

"Well, I hate to admit it, but I'm in a jam," Peter answered, flinging himself into a wicker chaise longue. "I need help."

"Gleeps, Peter, you sound desperate. What's up? You know you can always count on us," Trixie said.

"Oh, it's not a matter of life and death, so relax," he told them, smiling, "but I got a phone call just now from Brad Cummings. He and his brother are my regular crew. He told me they can't get down here until next week, because he has to take some kind of exam

for college, and the tune-up races are tomorrow morning. So. . . ."

"You don't mean you want *us* to go?" Trixie asked.
"We've only been out that once with you. We couldn't
possibly be any good in a regular race."

"In the first place, it isn't a regular race, so simmer
down," he told her. "It's just a warmer-upper. Besides,
from what Cap tells me and what I saw the other day,
all of you acted like able-bodied seamen, even if you
are new hands."

They all expressed their willingness to help out, and
Jim and Trixie were finally delegated to go with Peter.

"Trixie, you can handle the spinnaker, because you're
lighter than Jim and won't upset the balance of the
boat so much when you go forward to set the sail."
Peter was full of enthusiasm, but Trixie was still quite
apprehensive.

"The spinnaker! I've never even seen one outside a
sail bag, let alone put one up. I'd simply die if I didn't
do it right," she moaned.

"I'll tell you what," Peter said reassuringly. "We'll
go over to my house, and I'll show you a book that
describes the whole operation. It's really not difficult
at all—you'll see."

"May the rest of us come along, too?" Brian asked.
"We might as well learn the tricks of the trade while we
have a chance."

"Sure thing," Peter replied. "The more the merrier,

and we can look at the movies Dad took of some of the races last summer."

After taking their trays inside, they headed for Peter's house. By the end of the evening, Trixie felt a little more confident. As they were walking back to The Moorings, Jim gave her hand a reassuring squeeze.

"Don't worry, Trix; you can do anything you put your mind to. You know I think you're super!" he said.

For once in her life, Trixie was speechless. Her heart was racing. She thought, "I've just *got* to do it, not only to help Peter, but for Jim, too."

That night, although she went right to sleep, her rest was interrupted by a long series of dreams in which *Star Fire* capsized, because she stupidly hauled on the wrong line, or came in last, with everyone laughing at her vain attempts to hoist the spinnaker. But when dawn finally arrived, she felt less panicky and firmly resolved to keep her fears to herself.

Peter had proposed that they get to the club early in order to go out for a practice sail before race time. So he picked up Trixie and Jim, who had grabbed some breakfast on the run. The other Bob-Whites would come down later.

Peter looked up at the cloud-littered sky and remarked, "We've got a good breeze today, but it's a little out of the west, and the west wind is fickle."

"Is that a handicap?" Jim asked anxiously.

"No, not exactly," Peter replied. "It's fine when it's

blowing, but then, all of a sudden, no wind—usually just when you need it most to get across the finish line. Anyway, it'll be good practice."

After Peter had parked the Icebox, they brought the sail bags over to the lawn. Trixie and Jim spread out the huge, filmy spinnaker so Peter could fold and pack it properly in a cardboard carton. He pushed the two bottom corners, or feet, of the sail into the slots cut in the box so they could quickly and easily be snapped onto the sheets.

"It's not quite as complicated as folding a parachute, but almost." He chuckled as he finished the job and headed for the dock, Trixie and Jim following with the sail bags.

The club was almost deserted at this hour, and the launch wasn't yet running, so Peter borrowed a dinghy and rowed them out to the *Star Fire*, which was curtsying gaily at her mooring. The sails were soon hoisted, and, after sailing up to the dock to return the dinghy, they headed east into the bay.

"We're running before the wind now," Peter explained, "so we can set the spinny anytime. Are you ready to give it a try, Trix?"

"I'm as ready as I'll ever be." She climbed out of the cockpit and went forward, carrying the carton with her. She put the spinnaker pole in place on the mast, fastened the guy lines to the corners of the sail, and hoisted it. It filled almost immediately, and Trixie was so elated at her success that she forgot to take down the jib until Peter called to remind her.

"Jeepers, I forgot all about that," she yelled back as she hurriedly lowered the jib and left it in a neat pile on the deck ready to be hoisted again later on. She climbed back inside and, by carefully trimming the lines, kept the spinnaker well filled. *Star Fire* zoomed along at a merry clip, and Trixie was beginning to think that her fears had been rather silly and that the spinnaker detail was really pretty simple, after all, when suddenly the beautiful blue sail collapsed like a pricked balloon.

"Pete!" she cried. "I've forgotten what to do. Help me!"

"It's okay, Trix. Don't get all clutched up," Peter reassured her. "Remember, I said the wind was fickle. She's just showing you who's boss out here today."

Trixie saw that he was right. The wind had died, and they were barely moving.

"No knowing how long before the wind will be anything more than a breeze, so I guess we'd better take down the spinnaker and get back to the club, or we'll miss the start of the race," Peter suggested.

Luckily, by the time the jib was again in place, the wind freshened slightly and bore them back without difficulty. As they rounded the point and came in sight of the harbor, Trixie and Jim both let out a gasp of surprise. All the boats they had seen earlier bobbing

at their moorings now had their sails up. There were
about thirty in all.

"Gleeps!" cried Trixie. "Are they all going to race?
There'll be a traffic jam!"

They were near enough now to distinguish the various types of boats, and Peter explained that each kind
raced in its own class. He pointed out the little catboats,
called Wood Pussies, the Blue Jays, the Lightnings, and
the Stars. "Hey, there's the committee boat, and look
who's aboard. The Bob-Whites!" he yelled, waving to
a large motor cruiser. "That belongs to Cap's father.
They'll have a chance to watch the whole race. What
a break!"

At this point, a gun on the porch of the yacht club
went off, and Peter told them it signaled the start
of the Star race. "They're the biggest and fastest class
we have, and if they didn't go first, they'd run right
through the rest of us," he explained.

"Jeepers! What a sight!" Trixie cried as the eight
Stars, their sky-raking masts carrying a huge cloud of
sail, went careening up the bay.

"Lightnings next," Peter warned. "I set my stopwatch
when the gun for the Stars went off. Five minutes to
go!"

There were nine Lightnings besides *Star Fire* in the
race. Back and forth they went behind the line, jockey-
ing for the most advantageous position.

Trixie, her eyes shining with excitement, noticed

Blitzen sailing nearby. "Good luck, Cap," she called out with a wave of her hand.

"You, too," he yelled back good-naturedly.

Peter was now counting down for the start. "One minute to go," he intoned. "Fifty seconds, forty, thirty, twenty, ten, five. . . ."

Can I do it again? I just can't goof this time! Trixie thought, her heart pounding as the boats raced for the line.

Then Peter's voice broke in on her thoughts, "Four seconds to go, three, two, one—gun!"

They were off! The boats beat up the bay, well bunched, but *Star Fire* and *Blitzen* gradually drew ahead of the rest of the fleet, and Peter, looking behind him, said, "It looks like Cap's the one we'll have to beat. As soon as we round the harbor buoy, get set to fly the spinnaker, Trix, for the long run down to the next mark. Cap's really moving. Our only chance may be to outsmart him."

"Okay, Pete, I'll do my best," Trixie said fervently as she got ready to go up on the foredeck.

Star Fire and *Blitzen* were neck and neck as they approached the harbor buoy, which they had to round before heading out into the bay.

"All right, Trix, get ready to let her fly," Peter said, and, with a little prayer, Trixie climbed out of the cockpit, being careful not to upset the balance of the boat.

The lines, which at first glance looked completely

tangled, fell almost magically into place when she fixed
the guy lines to the spinnaker and started hoisting the
big blue sail. It filled beautifully, and *Star Fire* leaped
ahead as the balloon began to exert its terrific power.
This time Trixie remembered to take down the jib
before she dropped back into the boat.

"Good girl, Trix," Peter called out to her. "Cap's
spinny went up at least thirty seconds after yours."

Trixie hardly dared look around at first, but when
she finally stole a glance, she saw that *Star Fire* was
stealing away from *Blitzen* at an ever increasing rate.

"Hey, isn't Cap in trouble?" Jim suddenly cried. "I
don't think his spinnaker's filling, after all."

Peter, darting a look over his shoulder, said, "You're
right, Jim. His gear must have got fouled up somehow.
That's tough on Cap, but you know what they say: All's
fair in love and war—and boat racing!"

By this time, *Star Fire* had a commanding lead, and
she held it all the way to the black buoy, where they
had to come about before heading back to the finish
line. Cap finally got his boat moving again and, after
a few minutes, once more began to threaten *Star Fire*'s
lead. Trixie noticed that Peter's calm was giving way to
tension.

"Get ready to hoist the jib and take the spinny down,"
he ordered sharply, "and, Jim, trim the mains'l a bit as
we round the mark. Cap's coming up like greased lightning, and we can't afford to miss a trick!"

As *Star Fire* boiled up to the mark, Trixie raised the jib and clawed the spinnaker down. At the same moment, Jim trimmed the mainsail and Peter put the tiller hard over. They squeezed around the mark with only inches to spare and were off for the finish line.

"By Jove, that was perfect timing," Peter exulted. "You two are real pros!"

Trixie was tingling all over with the excitement of it all. She knew that one day she would have to have a boat of her own. There was nothing quite like sailing.

As Peter and Cap raced home, they met the rest of the fleet still making for the last mark, all of them seeming very slow compared to the two lead boats. *Blitzen* had cut down on *Star Fire*'s lead until now no more than fifty feet separated them. The tension was almost unbearable. Peter, crouched over the tiller, glanced up at the sails every few seconds to be sure they were filled, but not once did he look back.

Suddenly Trixie said, "Pete, I do believe the wind is getting fluky again, like it was earlier this morning."

"You're right, old girl," he crowed. "It just may haul around, and if it does, we may have time to use the spinny again. Let's get it ready, anyway. Try not to let Cap see you go forward, so he won't catch on to our little plan."

Cap apparently didn't notice the activity on *Star Fire*. Peter kept his eyes on the water to watch for any ripple that would indicate a shift in the wind. Sure enough, before very long it got very puffy, and Jim and Peter had a hard time keeping the sails full and drawing. Then it settled down to a steady blow from behind them.

"Spinnaker!" Peter yelled as he saw his hunch was right. Trixie had the sail up in a flash. *Star Fire* leaped again and rushed for the finish line.

"We've got him!" Peter shouted exultantly. "We caught old Cap napping!"

He was right. Cap had missed the trick. He had been so intent on overtaking *Star Fire,* he hadn't noticed how variable the wind had become, so his crew wasn't ready to take advantage of it as Peter had done. When he saw Peter's strategy, his crew tried frantically to get the huge sail up, but it was too late. *Star Fire* raced across the line, and the gun, signaling the winner, roared again from the club.

Before its echoes had died, Trixie, Peter, and Jim began yelling and laughing and slapping each other on the back.

"Jeepers!" Trixie cried. "I'll never, *never* be the same again!"

"What a race!" Jim yelled.

"And what a crew!" Peter added. "Trix, I've said it once, and I'll say it again: You're absolutely super."

"You can say *that* again," Jim said seriously. Trixie felt unexpected tears rising. She tried to laugh off their praise as she started to get the sails down.

"Now I know what they mean when people talk about tears of joy," she said to herself, "but I don't know whether mine are because we won or because of what Peter and Jim said. Or do I?"

Another Clue · 14

EVERYONE CROWDED AROUND to congratulate Peter as he walked up the dock, and he was not slow in giving his crew a big share of the credit. Jim and Trixie found themselves the center of a crowd of admirers as they went up on the porch where sandwiches and soft drinks were being served. Cap, in particular, sought them out to tell them what a fine job they had done.

"Don't let my crew hear me," he whispered good-naturedly to Pete, "but they aren't as good as Jim and Trixie, and they've been racing with me for three years."

"Oh, we were just lucky," Trixie said. "You know what they say about beginners, and, besides, Peter really made it all seem so easy."

The other Bob-Whites soon joined them, and after they had finished eating, they said good-bye to Cap and the others and headed for the Icebox.

176

"Why don't you stick around for a while?" Cap urged. "We might get up a game of tennis."

"It sounds tempting, Cap," Trixie replied, "but we've just got to go and see El. We haven't had a minute since he broke his leg. See you later, and I hope we can get together for a game before we leave."

Elmer lived in a neat little cottage near the center of the island. As they drove up to the curb, Brian asked, "Don't you think maybe just one of us should go to the door and inquire how he is first? He might not want all seven of us barging in at once."

"Why don't you go?" Honey suggested. "After all, you're the one who really took care of him when he had the accident."

"Okay," Brian agreed. He jumped out of the car and ran down the brick path to the front door. Soon after he rapped the little anchor knocker, the door was opened by a stout, pleasant woman in an attractive housedress and a big white apron.

Brian had no sooner introduced himself than Mrs. Thomas said El had seen him coming and wanted all of them to come right in. She hustled Brian inside and was off down the path, taking her apron off as she went, to tell the others they should all go right in and see her husband.

"Land sakes, El hasn't talked about another thing since he got hurt but how you helped him. He was hoping you'd come by, but he knows how busy you young folks are, being here such a short time and all."

Although the cottage looked quite small from the outside, the living room was spacious, and the Bob-Whites, after greeting El, were invited to "sit a spell."

"It'll do El so much good to have visitors. He gets restless, not being able to get out and around like he's used to," Mrs. Thomas said as she brought in an extra chair from the dining room.

There was much to tell El about the fallen tree, the work of cleaning after the storm, and their meeting with Peter.

"Well, I'll be back on the job in a few more weeks," El said. "Doc says I'm making fine progress. You know, this is the first time I've been laid up since I started taking care of The Moorings."

"When was that?" Trixie asked him, more to make conversation than out of any real curiosity.

"Well, let's see now. It was about five years before Mr. Condon died, and he's been gone eighteen or nineteen years, so it's close to a quarter century since I started in as yard boy."

Trixie's ears pricked up, and she saw, as she glanced at Jim and the others, that they had imperceptibly leaned forward as El spoke.

"I was just a young shaver then, and I didn't care too much for work," El continued with a smile, "but Mr. C, as we all called him, was as patient a man as

I've ever met. He got me interested in gardening, and 'fore I knew it, I was actually looking forward to going to work. I even started to read up on shrubs and pruning and stuff like that, so I could do a good job."

"You certainly have made the place beautiful," Trixie said. "Did you ever work on Mr. Condon's boat? I saw a picture of it down at the club the other day."

"No, it's funny, but I never took to the sea, even though I was born and bred right here on this island and my grandfather was a whaler. It was my buddy, Ed, who was the sailor, and he went out on *Sapphire* every chance he could, until Mr. C's heart got so bad he had to quit sailing. But, you know," El continued reminiscently, "Mr. C never gave up to his illness. No, sir, he went out for walks every day, and Ed often went with him for company.

"They even worked out some kind of sailing game to entertain them on the way. Ed used to laugh at me because I never could get the hang of it, but he and Mr. C used to get a lot of fun out of figuring the courses they set up."

"You said Ed was the sailor. Did he give it up, too, when Mr. Condon got sick?" Jim asked.

El's head lowered, and it was obviously an effort for him to continue the story, but he went on. "No, you see, my friend was lost at sea off a bunker boat, and Mr. C died a day or so after he heard that Ed was gone."

"How terrible!" Trixie exclaimed.

"Well, it was awful hard on me," El continued, "but the ones it really hit were Ethel and the baby. Ed had got married a couple of years before. That's how he came to go out on the bunker boats. He had to earn more than he'd been making doing odd jobs and such."

"Whatever happened to his wife and baby?" Jim inquired solicitously.

"She couldn't stand living here anymore after Ed went, so she moved South-side. There was enough insurance money from the company that owned the boats to take care of them until the youngster went to school, and then Ethel started selling baked stuff—bread and muffins and cakes—and, you know, before long she'd built up enough business so she couldn't handle it all from her home, and she opened up a little shop."

"She must have been a wonderful person," commented Honey.

"Are you talking about Ethel?" Mrs. Thomas asked as she came in from the kitchen with a plate of freshly baked cookies. "She's one in a million, and her son, too. I get a card from them every Christmas."

Her cheerful presence broke the spell of sadness which had settled over the room. "Now, help yourself. I just made this batch this morning. It's a new recipe, and I'm not sure they're fit to eat," she chattered on as she passed the plate. "My grandchildren like me to make different kinds. They live right next door, and I have to keep the cookie jar full for their visits."

"Never knew you to make a poor cookie—or anything else, for that matter," El told her as he took a generous handful. "She's the best cook on Cobbett's Island."

Everyone agreed that the cookies were delicious, and Mrs. Thomas beamed as she saw the last one disappear. After thanking her and assuring El that all was going well at The Moorings, the Bob-Whites said good-bye.

They had no sooner climbed into the Icebox than everyone started to talk at once. Now that Ed's family had become a reality, they were more than ever determined to find out if there was anything to the mystery of the hidden money.

"What did El mean by South-side?" Trixie asked Peter.

"That's the way the islanders speak of the southern point of Long Island. It could be that Ethel lives anywhere from Montauk to Southampton," Peter answered.

"Do you suppose the telephone directory would give us a lead?" suggested Brian.

"It might, if we knew Ed's last name," Trixie said impatiently. "Do you realize that, with all the information we've managed to get, we still don't know *that?*"

"I know, and it would have seemed kind of obvious if we'd asked El," Jim added.

"Say, wait a minute," Trixie cried, snapping her fingers. "Di, if you were going to open up a bakeshop, what would you call it?"

"I'd call it the Calorie Emporium," Mart interrupted.

"Oh, stop it, Mart. I'm serious," Trixie said.

"I suppose I'd call it Diana's Bake Shoppe, just to be quaint," Di replied. "Why?"

"I get the idea!" said Mart gleefully. "Ethel's Bake-shop. Am I right, Trix?"

"Jeepers, Mart, you're getting to be a real sleuth. Maybe we'll have to let you into the firm." Trixie's eyes twinkled as she replied. "That's exactly what I was thinking. Hurry up, Peter; let's stop at The Moorings and look it up."

They nearly fell over each other in their rush to get at the directory on the hall table. Trixie took it out on the porch, and while everyone waited breathlessly, she looked in the Yellow Pages under "Bakeries—Retail." Jim, who was leaning over her shoulder, was the first to spot the advertisement for Ethel's Bakery. "You're right, Trixie," he cried. "At least, there is an Ethel. Now we'll have to find out if she's the one we're looking for."

"Yippee!" exclaimed Mart. "Where does she live?"

"Let's see," Trixie said as she read on. " 'Ethel's Bakery. Mrs. Ethel Hall, proprietor. Homemade bread, rolls, and pastries. Cakes for all occasions. JU-nine-one thousand. Locust Lane, Easthampton.' "

"That must be the right one," Mart said. "Now all we lack is the thousand dollars."

"Oh, Trixie, if only, if only—" moaned Honey.

"You're so right," Trixie answered. "If only we could

break the secret of the chart. It *must* mean something. I feel so helpless, I could scream!"

"Brian, you seem lost in thought. What's on your mind?" Peter asked.

"I was just wondering what kind of a game it was that Mr. C and Ed used to play," he replied. "Isn't there one that involves sailing or boats or something?"

"There's one you play with model boats, I think," Peter answered, "but I've never seen it. It would be fun to try and work one out, wouldn't it?"

Trixie, who had been only half listening to the boys' conversation, suddenly jumped up from the hammock and dashed into the house.

"Now, what do you suppose has gotten into her this time?" Mart asked as he followed her inside, for even though he often teased his almost-twin to the point of distraction, he was always secretly concerned when he felt she was worried or discouraged.

"My guess is that she's had one of her hunches," Jim remarked. "Wait and see. I'll bet she'll be right back in a minute."

He was right. It wasn't long before Trixie came back, carrying the chart with her. She spread it out on the table and began to study it intently.

"Gosh, Trix, you must know that thing by heart now," said Mart, who had also rejoined the group. "What's up?"

"Jim, run in and get the letter, will you? I forgot it,

and I want to look at it again. It's on the desk in the library," said Trixie, ignoring Mart's question.

"Sure thing, but you must know the letter by heart, too, Trix," Jim said as he went into the house.

"I know it all sounds silly, but I may have found the last piece in our puzzle, so step on it," she said, her voice tense.

As they were waiting for Jim to come back, Honey glanced at the chart and again hummed the six elusive notes. "I wish I could get a hunch about that little puzzler," she said, "because I just know it has something to do with the whole thing."

"It's been running through my head all week," Mart added. "Maybe it's from some old song that was popular in Ed's day."

Jim came back with the letter and handed it to Trixie. They all watched her while she read it through once again. Then, speaking very slowly, she said, "Okay, here's my theory. See what you think of it. Remember what El said about Mr. C working out a kind of game with Ed? Well, since they couldn't go out on *Sapphire* anymore, maybe the game was a sailing game, like Brian mentioned, laid around the neighborhood, where they took their walks. Does that make any sense?"

"I don't quite see it," said Jim, scratching his head. "Why put the buoy mark on the chart if it's a land course? Wouldn't it be simpler just to put down a tree or a rock or whatever?"

"Sure, it would be simpler, but it wouldn't be half as much fun or take half as many brains to figure out that kind of map," Mart answered loftily.

"Well, it's a possibility," Honey answered, a little skeptical. "It won't do any harm to explore it. Everything else has led to a dead end. But why were you so interested in the letter?"

"Look here a minute," said Trixie quickly, beckoning Honey to the table. "Notice how Ed has set off the words 'start sailing' in quotation marks? Why would he do that if he really meant sailing? I think it's a cue to follow the course on land instead of on sea."

"By Jove, I think you've got something there!" Peter exclaimed. "Let's have a look at the chart. Now, let's assume that they started out from the same place on the porch that we did the first time when we plotted our course to the gazebo."

Everyone raced around to the other side of the porch, led by Trixie, carrying the chart and the letter. She jumped up onto the railing and, looking toward Peter's house, let out a delighted scream. "There it is! The spire! It's the one on the gazebo!"

Jim caught her as she jumped down and spun her around and around, while the others joined in what looked like an impromptu war dance.

Just as they were about to head for the gazebo, Celia came out to announce lunch. "Oh, jeepers, do we have to eat?" cried Trixie.

"No, but if you don't, you'll miss your favorite dish, macaroni and cheese," Celia answered.

"Mac-a-chee!" yelled Mart. "Not on your life we don't miss lunch."

"Our compliments to the chef, and we'll be in in a minute," Honey said. She invited Peter to stay, but he explained that he had to go off the island that afternoon to get some plants that his mother had ordered from a nursery in Amagansett.

"Gosh, I'd much rather stay here," he said dismally. "Now I'll miss all the fun of testing Trixie's theory."

"You won't miss a thing," Trixie quickly reassured him. "We wouldn't think of going on without you. We'll wait until tomorrow morning, so we'll have a whole free day."

Peter started to protest, but all the other Bob-Whites agreed with Trixie that the project should be postponed.

"Say, why don't you all come along with me, then?" Peter suggested. "I have to go right through Easthampton, and we can stop at Ethel's Bakery."

"Wonderful!" Trixie agreed enthusiastically. "Maybe we'll get some leads if we go in to buy something and get chatty with whoever waits on us."

"I'm a great customer in a bakery," Mart remarked. "I can taste those ephemeral doughnuts now."

"Ephemeral?" Jim repeated quizzically.

"Yes, it means anything that's short-lived or lasts only a day, and when I'm around, jelly doughnuts are sure ephemeral," Mart chuckled.

Everyone groaned loudly at Mart's attempted wit.

"You go ahead and have lunch, and I'll go home and grab a sandwich while I go over the list of stuff I'm supposed to get with Mother," Peter said. "She's going to let me take the station wagon, so there'll be plenty of room for us and the plants, too. See you pronto!" He hurdled the low porch railing and dashed home as the Bob-Whites went in to lunch.

This time, instead of taking the Greenpoint ferry, they drove to the south side of the island and boarded a smaller ferry that carried them over the narrow sound to the mainland. The trip took only a few minutes, and then they were on their way to Easthampton.

"Maybe we'd better go right on to the nursery and pick up the plants. Then we won't have to worry about time," suggested Peter in his usual well-organized way. "There might even be time to visit the Whaling Museum in Sag Harbor on the way home."

"Oh, I hope there'll be time," Trixie said. "You know, we usually have to write something interesting about our vacations for English class, and that would make a wonderful theme."

"If any of us wrote about our search for the missing money, no one would believe us," Mart said. "They'd think we dreamed the whole thing."

As they drove slowly along the beautiful main street of Easthampton, with its canopy of ancient elm trees, they were all on the lookout for Locust Lane. "There it is, off to the left," cried Trixie, pointing to a narrow, winding street. "Step on it, Pete. I'm dying to get back and see if that's the right place."

"Patience, Trix, old girl. I'm going as fast as the city fathers will allow," Peter replied cheerfully. "You don't want me to get a ticket, do you?"

When they arrived at the nursery and Peter was conferring about his mother's order, Trixie and the others wandered around outside the main building, where the owner had laid out a typical Japanese garden. They noticed charming little odd-shaped pools, edged with unusual plants and crossed by miniature arched bridges or a series of artistically shaped stepping-stones. Water flowed from pool to pool over half-concealed waterfalls. As they followed the winding paths, they came upon stone ornaments, some in the shapes of birds or animals. Lanterns and benches along the way seemed to invite them to stop and rest. A weeping flowering crab tree was in full bloom, its graceful boughs dipping into the water.

"Oh, I feel as though I were really in Japan!" Honey exclaimed as she stopped in front of one of the statues. "Wouldn't it be fun to have a garden like this at home? Down near the weeping willow by the lake would be a perfect place for one. I think I'll read up on Japanese gardens and ask Mother to let me plan one."

Peter came out with the proprietor just in time to

hear Honey's enthusiastic proposal.

"I agree they *are* fascinating, but let me warn you: Don't choose it as a do-it-yourself project unless you have endless patience," the man said. "Many of these little trees and plants are very old. They have been pruned and shaped for years to give just the effect the gardener wants."

"That wouldn't be a hobby for me, then," Trixie broke in. "Patience isn't my strongest virtue."

"Oh, I don't know," Jim remarked. "You sure have stick-to-itiveness, and that's just patience plus positive action, isn't it?"

"That sure sounds impressive, Jim, but I'm afraid it's just stubborn old bullheadedness," Trixie replied. "Once I get on the trail of something mysterious, I just can't bear to give up."

When the plants had been loaded into the station wagon, Honey told the nursery owner how much they had enjoyed the few minutes spent in his beautiful garden.

"If you have a moment before you go, let me point out something you may have missed," he said, leading them to a spot nearby. "The tendency seems to be for visitors in an oriental garden to look down instead of up, but just glance into the top of that big maple tree at the edge of the garden. Do you see anything special?"

"Why, yes," Trixie cried. "I see the outline of a woman, a little Japanese woman in a kimono, right where that big branch comes out of the main trunk."

"I see it, too," Honey exclaimed, "and it looks as though her hands were folded into the sleeves of her dress!"

"And her head is bowed as though she were thinking," added Diana.

"That's right," the nurseryman answered, pleased at their perceptiveness. "Do you boys see the little goddess?" he asked, turning to them.

After they, too, had identified the lifelike branch, he told them that the Oriental loves to discover, in trees or rocks, forms that resemble people, animals, or birds. "I was lucky enough to spot that little lady. Her silhouette shows up only from this particular vantage point. So, as my Japanese friends would do, I set up this little shrine in her honor. We call her the Lady of the Treetops."

"She's charming, and so is her shrine," Honey said as they admired the delicate miniature pagoda. "Thanks so much for letting us see her."

"And hereafter we'll remember to look up as well as down when we visit a Japanese garden," Trixie added.

"Well, it's something for you young people to think about," the nurseryman said as they walked back to the car. "No matter where you are, don't forget to look up."

Jelly Doughnuts • 15

It DIDN'T TAKE LONG to get back to Easthampton and Locust Lane. As Peter drove around the first turn in the road, Trixie caught sight of a sign near the curb, painted to look like a large birthday cake, with ETHEL'S BAKERY lettered on the side. They parked in front of the small two-storied building which was set a little back from the street. On the ground floor, a large bay window with crisp white curtains was filled with an assortment of cookies, buns, cakes, and pies.

"I'll bet Ethel lives upstairs," said Trixie as they walked up the gravel path to the shop. "Doesn't it look like there's an apartment up there?"

"I'm sure she does," said Mart, tearing himself away from the tempting display in the window long enough to read the nameplate on the door to the upper floor. "It says 'Mrs. Edward Hall.'"

"My legs are shaking like leaves," Trixie confessed.

As she opened the door, a little brass bell tinkled overhead, and an aroma of "sugar and spice and everything nice" made their mouths water. Two customers were ahead of them, and, with only one person behind the counter, there was time to look around the little shop. Its spotless white walls were decorated simply with a few beautiful old blue and white plates. A bouquet of mixed flowers stood on a table opposite the bay window, and glass-fronted cabinets filled with baked goods occupied the other two sides. Behind the counter was a cheery-looking woman in a blue and white striped dress, her graying hair braided in a coronet around her head. Trixie noticed that she was full of chitchat, exchanging bits of local gossip and inquiring about this one and that one as she filled the orders.

"Now, what can I do for you young folks?" she asked pleasantly when the other customers had finally left.

"We really don't know *what* we want, everything looks so good, although my brother did mention jelly doughnuts," Trixie said with a smile.

"What boy doesn't like jelly doughnuts?" The woman laughed. "Why, my son would eat them practically by the dozen. If I hadn't put my foot down, he would have eaten up all my profits!"

"And look at those adorable gingerbread men!" cried Diana. "Why don't we take some home to Bobby and the twins?" she asked, turning to Trixie.

"Gleeps! I remember now that I promised Bobby I'd bring him a present, and I probably won't have a chance to get a game or anything for him before we go home. These will be perfect. I'll take two of them, please, Mrs.—" Trixie paused expectantly.

"Hall, my dear, but most folks just call me Ethel. I said to myself when you came in that you weren't from around here," she chattered on. "Being in the shop as long as I have, I know just about everyone in town and most of the summer people, too."

"Actually, all of us, except Peter here, are from Sleepyside, up in Westchester," Brian said. "We've been over on Cobbett's Island for a week or so, but we wanted to see Easthampton and Sag Harbor before we went home."

Trixie, who was watching Mrs. Hall intently, noticed an expression of sadness cross her face as she lowered her head.

"I used to know Cobbett's Island real well," she said. "As a matter of fact, I was born and raised there." She hesitated. "Yes, and married there, too."

"We love the island," Honey exclaimed. "I can't imagine why anyone would ever want to leave it. It's so beautiful!"

"I loved it, too, and it holds wonderful memories for me, but memories can be painful, as you know. Oh, what am I saying? You're all too young to have anything but bright memories." She was smiling again.

"I think I know what you mean," Jim said. "I lost both my parents when I was just a little kid, so my childhood was pretty grim, but I try not to think about it any more than I can help."

"That's right, young man; no use dwelling on the past, I always say. That's why I came over here after I lost my husband, to make a new life for myself and my boy."

"Well, from the looks of this lovely little shop, I'd say you had succeeded," Trixie said, looking around admiringly. "Do you do all the baking yourself?"

"I used to when Eddie was home to help wait on customers, but when he went off to college, I had to get someone to help me. But I still do all the special cakes and such," she said with a touch of pride.

"Is your son coming back here after college?" asked Mart. "I can't think of a pleasanter business, and, by the way, I'll take a dozen jelly doughnuts, please."

"Mercy, no," Mrs. Hall answered as she packed the doughnuts in a cardboard box. "It's never been anything but medicine for him. He's dreamed of being a doctor from the time he was just a little tyke, and now he has one more year to go. It's been a struggle, but he's made it this far."

"That's what I'm aiming for, too. I've always wanted to be a doctor," Brian said. "I know how he feels."

"Well, it's a fine ambition, but be prepared for years of hard work and some disappointments, too." Mrs.

Hall nodded slowly, and her face clouded.

"What do you mean 'disappointments'?" asked Trixie, sensing that Eddie's mother had something special in mind.

"Well, you take my boy. He has one more year, as I was saying, and a partial scholarship. I help out with what I can, but this year his schedule is so heavy he won't be able to take odd jobs to earn his living expenses." She paused, then finally continued, "He's just about decided to take a year off to earn the money and then go back."

"Oh, that would be a shame, losing a whole year!" exclaimed Trixie. "Isn't there any other way?"

"He could borrow the money, but he won't go into debt, and I can't say I blame him. My husband always said we should keep clear of debt, and I've taught Eddie the same thing. Here's his picture," she said proudly, opening a little gold locket and removing it from a chain around her neck.

"He's really good-looking!" exclaimed Diana as she passed the locket around for the others to see.

"He's the image of his father when he was the same age," Mrs. Hall continued. She reached behind her and, from a drawer under one of the cabinets, brought out a faded photograph and passed it over the counter for them to see. She glanced at it lovingly.

"Yes, that's my Ed," she added sadly. "He was lost at sea when Eddie was just a baby, so my boy never knew him, but they're a lot alike."

The bell over the door rang again, announcing another customer, so after deciding on an assortment of cookies and some brownies to eat on the way home, they bade Mrs. Hall good-bye and started to leave.

"Do come back again," she said, and then, calling to Brian, she added, "By the way, if you want to know more about medical school, drop in and talk to Eddie. He's coming home tomorrow for a few days between exams."

"Thanks a lot, Mrs. Hall," Brian replied. "I'd like nothing better."

"And bring all your friends," she added cordially.

Trixie could hardly wait to get into the car before her excitement broke forth. "That's Ed's wife, all right, and she couldn't be nicer! We've just *got* to find the money, or I'll—"

"Or you'll what, Trix?" Diana asked with a smile.

"Oh, you know, Di," Trixie answered. "I'll simply die!"

"In addition to being the means of saving Trixie's life, can you imagine what a thousand dollars would mean to Ethel and Eddie?" Mart commented.

"It couldn't come at a better time," Peter added. "Let's hope we're lucky."

"We'll need more than luck, I'm afraid," Trixie sighed. "We'll need the brains of every B.W.G. member, and you, too, Peter. Tomorrow's our last chance!"

As they were leaving Easthampton, Peter pointed out an old weathered, shingled saltbox house overlooking the village green and pond. "That's the boyhood home of John Payne, who wrote 'Home, Sweet Home,' and the house next to it was built by old Fishhook Mulford. They say that when he went to England to protest the tax on whale oil, he heard there were a lot of pickpockets in London. So what did he do but line his pockets with fishhooks! No one seems to know how he got his *own* money out, but it makes a good story, anyway."

When they got to Sag Harbor, Trixie checked her wristwatch and found it was only four thirty, so there was time to stop at the Whaling Museum before going back to Cobbett's Island.

The large, square, white building had been designed originally as a private home, and, like so many residences built in the mid-1800's, it showed the influence of Greek architecture in the two-storied Corinthian columns and the decorative moldings. The enormous jawbone of a whale had been set up to arch the main doorway when the building was converted to a museum. Once inside, the Bob-Whites scattered through the various rooms, the girls more interested in the collection of antique dolls, household utensils, and clothes than the boys, who spent more time examining the harpoons, scrimshaw work, ship models, and pictures of the whaling trade. There was so much to see that they were

all surprised when the custodian told them it was
closing time.

"Jeepers!" Trixie exclaimed as they were heading
home. "We've got enough material for sixty school
papers, just from what we've seen today."

"Maybe next year you can manage to improve your
English marks without running to me for help, dear
sister," Mart quipped.

"Oh, I could *never* do without my walking encyclopedia," Trixie chuckled. "Please don't desert me now!"

The Chart and the Compass • 16

WHEN TRIXIE AWOKE the next morning, it was quite dark in her room. She looked at the little clock on the bedside table and was surprised to see it was already eight thirty. Di was still sleeping soundly, so Trixie tiptoed to the window and quietly pulled back the curtains. Then she understood why the room had seemed so shadowy and dim. A thick fog hung over the harbor and enveloped the house. It was so dense that she couldn't see the dock across the road or even the hedge in front of the house.

"Jeepers!" she said to herself. "This is fine weather for trying to follow a chart on land *or* sea."

When she heard Honey stirring in the adjoining room, she went in to tell her the sad news about the weather. "And do you realize that tomorrow is the day we're supposed to leave for home?" Trixie reminded her. "So it's now or never, no matter what the weather. Come on, lazybones; get a move on!"

Honey sat up in bed and stretched her arms high above her head, muttering through a yawn, "Who was it who said this was going to be a quiet vacation?"

Trixie laughingly threw a pillow at her and went to wake Diana and the boys.

"Well, as the plot thickens, so does the fog," Mart chuckled as they met for breakfast. "Do you intend to pursue your will-o'-the-wisp in this weather, dear leader?" he asked his sister.

"It's not the least bit will-o'-the-wispish, Mart Belden," snapped Trixie angrily, "and if you don't want to help, you don't have to. You can drop out right now!"

"Oh, you know he won't quit," said Diana, quickly coming to Mart's defense. "You ought to be used to his teasing by now, Trix."

"Oh, I'm used to it, all right, and you know—" she paused, thought a minute, and then continued, "the reason I get mad is probably because sometimes his remarks have a grain of truth in them that I've refused to face up to."

As she said this, she smiled fondly at her brother. Mart was so surprised at this unaccustomed response that he dropped his fork and was glad of an excuse to dive under the table to retrieve it.

"You don't mean you think we're foolish to keep looking, do you, Trix?" Jim asked apprehensively.

"No, of course not. It's just that—well, we mustn't let ourselves expect too much, or we'll be awfully disappointed if we don't find the money. You know, today is our last day," Trixie pointed out.

"Well, then, let's get on with it and hope our efforts pay off," suggested Brian.

After breakfast, as Honey was phoning Peter that they were on their way, Trixie called out, "Tell him to bring a compass, if he has one. We may need it."

"We'd better take a flashlight so we won't get run down—if anyone is foolish enough to drive in this pea soup," added Jim.

"Well, I can see my hand in front of my face, but that's about all," said Honey as they went outside.

"Just follow along the hedge, and we'll soon come to Pete's gate," said Jim, taking the lead.

"Righto, old chap," Mart said in his best imitation of an English accent. "This is just like jolly old England. Chin up. Pip, pip!"

Peter was waiting for them near the entrance to the garden, and together they slowly made their way toward the gazebo. "This fog will probably burn off in a few hours," he said hopefully. "It's a good thing we haven't got a race scheduled today."

"It doesn't help us any, either, but it certainly lends a ghostly atmosphere," Honey said with a shiver. "Where do we go from here?"

"The next mark after the spire is the rock, and it's

southwest from here," Trixie noted, "but it doesn't say
how far."

"Maybe it's one of the stones in the slave cemetery,"
Diana suggested. "What direction would that be?"

"I'm afraid that's too far north," said Peter, "because
they're over near the gate, back of us."

"Let's follow the compass southwest, and we may
bump into something," suggested Trixie, impatient to
get started.

They had gone only a short distance when Brian, who
was in the lead, almost fell over the same stone on which
they had broken the bottle a few days before. "Oh, no!
How stupid can we get?" cried Trixie. "Why didn't
someone *think* of this? It's so *obvious!*"

"That's probably why," Mart said. "We were all looking for something more elusive."

"You can be sure the black buoy will be more elusive,"
Peter sighed, "because I'm dead sure there aren't any
black buoys to stumble over anywhere around here." He
consulted the chart, which Trixie was carrying, and
then started out due south.

"Jeepers! This is taking us right back into the jungle,"
Trixie said as they slowly worked their way through the
tangle of vines. "Is there anything back in there, Pete?"

"Nothing but an old smokehouse, where they used
to cure hams and bacon," Peter answered. "I found it
when we first came here, but I haven't been near it
since. It's pretty ramshackle."

"A smokehouse—smoke, soot, black, *black buoy,*" Trixie muttered to herself. Then suddenly she cried, "I'll bet you anything the smokehouse is our next mark. Keep going!"

"It's lucky we wore our foul-weather gear, or we'd never get through these brambles," Brian said as he pushed aside the clinging canes from the old raspberry bushes.

They had penetrated the thicket for about two hundred feet when they came to the little shanty, which was in line with the compass marking.

"How long did you say it's been since you were here, Pete?" asked Trixie, her brows furrowing, as she started to look around.

"About two years, I'd say. Why?" he answered.

"Well, someone's been here not more than two *days* ago," Trixie rejoined. "Look at the vines around the door. They've all been pulled down, and recently, too. See where these new shoots have been pulled off the main stem?"

"And look here, Trix," Honey cried. "There's a fresh semicircle on the ground where the door was pulled open!"

"But they couldn't have come the way we did, or we would have seen their trail," Diana said.

"Maybe they came in from another direction," volunteered Mart, going around to the other side of the smokehouse. "See here, where the vines are trampled down," he called out as he pointed to an opening in the underbrush.

"I think you're right, Mart, but why do you say 'they'?" Trixie inquired as she went back and poked her head inside the door. She had taken the flashlight from Jim and was shining it on the floor. "It was only *one* person, or I miss my guess. Look at these footprints!"

"Golly, you're right, Trix," said Jim, looking over her shoulder. "Only one pair shows up in the dust, and they look as though they were made by worn-out sneakers."

In a corner Trixie caught sight of a black jacket that had obviously been thrown down very recently. "Now I'm positive that our mysterious guest in the toolshed is the same one we saw from the attic. He probably helped himself to Peter's chart and has beat us to this mark. If we don't hurry," she said, "this is one race we may not win!"

By now the sun was beginning to break through the fog, making their progress somewhat easier. After they came out into the open, they headed southeast across an open field, on the far side of which was the lily pool. Honey, wiping her damp forehead, suggested they stop there for a breather before going on.

"And let's get out of these slickers," Diana added, stripping off her coat. "I'm simply dying of the heat!"

"Where, oh, where are you, red nun?" Trixie wailed as she sat down on one of the stone benches, shading her eyes with her hand and looking all around.

"The only red thing I see around here is that rambler rose over by the statue," said Mart, "and there's nothing southeast of here except the vegetable gardens and the wall."

"Gleeps!" cried Trixie, jumping to her feet. "The statue! Doesn't she look something like a nun with that veil on her head? I'll bet she's the gal we're looking for!"

"Or the buoy," punned Mart, elated at having provided a clue to the course.

"That climbing rose is years old," commented Peter, "so it could have been here when Ed and Mr. C were alive. Good work, Trixie; let's get going."

Everyone soon forgot the uncomfortable humidity and eagerly started out again behind the lily pool.

"This is the longest leg of the course, if the distances between marks on the chart mean anything," Trixie commented.

"And it's the last one, thank goodness," Honey added, "but there aren't any clues to help us this time; just the word 'Finish.'"

"Any ideas, Pete?" Jim asked. "What are those buildings way down at the far end of the field, near the woods?"

"The big gray one is the stable. The funny-shaped one on the right is the corncrib, and that one over there is the base of the old windmill. The wings got blown off before we came," Peter said, pointing out the various structures.

"Well, the stable is right plumb in our path if this compass is right, so we'll have to look through it. But where do you start in a big old ark like that?" said Trixie, throwing up her hands in despair.

"It's like hunting for a needle in a haystack," said Mart as they approached the stable.

They pushed open the wide double doors to get as much light as possible and stepped into the murky interior of the old building. As their eyes got used to the half-light, they saw harnesses and halters still hanging on their pegs along one side, and in the back of the stable, Honey discovered an old sleigh.

"Look at this adorable old sleigh," she called to the others as she climbed in.

Brian jumped in beside her and, pretending to take the reins, started to sing. " 'Oh, what fun it is to ride in a one-horse open sleigh!' " The others joined in lustily.

On the other side of the main room of the stable were the stalls, three for regular-sized horses, and another smaller one, which Jim guessed was for a pony or a colt. The names of the long-ago occupants were painted in quaint letters above the stalls: GALLANT BOY, DIAMOND, POPCORN, and over the fourth, NOEL.

"I'll bet Noel was a Christmas present for one of your great-aunts or great-uncles," mused Trixie. "I wonder what color she was."

"Look at this cute little food box in here, just high enough for a little pony to feed from," called Diana, who had been looking around inside the smallest stall.

"That's called a manger, not a food box, silly." Mart laughed. "It comes from the French verb *manger*, 'to eat.' "

"Okay, manger," Diana answered good-naturedly. "Away in a manger, Noel ate her hay," she sang, parodying the old Christmas carol.

Just then Trixie let out a shriek and repeated the first bar. "Da-dum-da-da-dum-dum. Honey, wasn't that the tune on the chart?" she asked breathlessly.

When Honey and Mart whistled the melody again, it was obvious that Trixie was right. Dashing into the stall, she flashed the light into the manger and started pulling out the hay that still remained in it. She noticed that one of the boards on the bottom had two holes bored in it, and, sticking her fingers into them, she was able to lift it out easily. Underneath was a small black tin box!

Everyone was so tense with expectancy that it was not until Trixie had gingerly carried the box over to the light and lifted the cover that anyone made a sound. But when they saw a neatly tied bundle of bills, their excitement erupted, and they whooped and hollered as they danced around the box on the floor.

Their elation was abruptly cut short when they heard a loud thud and a voice yelling at them from the

rear of the stable. "Okay, you guys, pipe down. Do
you want the whole island to get wise?"

Whirling around in the direction of the voice, they
saw a sullen-looking boy advancing toward them, a gun
in his hand. His face was distorted. His T-shirt was torn
and filthy, and Trixie noticed, as her eyes swept from
his head to his feet, that his arms and legs were badly
scratched and that he was wearing dirty white sneakers.

"Now, just line up there along the wall, sailors, and
we'll talk this whole thing over, like one big, happy
family," he continued with sarcastic politeness.

Mart started toward him, fists doubled, but Peter,
yelling, "Get back, all of you!" pushed him back before
he had time to protest. The others silently lined up, as
they had been ordered to. There seemed no alternative
—not with a revolver covering them!

"Attaboy, Pete," snarled the stranger. "You've got
sense enough to know I ain't foolin', and the rest of
you better get wise, too." He spun the revolver around
on his index finger a couple of times, then deftly brought
it back into shooting position.

"Now, like I was sayin'," he continued, striding up
and down in front of them, "I seen you steal that box
from the stall. I was up in the loft and had a good
view right through that there hole in the ceiling where
they pitch the hay down for the horses. Looks like
there's quite a nice little bundle here"—he took the
money out of the box with his left hand—"and, man,

that's what I need. I'm gonna make a deal with you!"
His eyes narrowed, and he looked from one to the
other. "What d'ya say, chums?"

"Let's hear your offer, pal," Trixie quickly answered,
tossing her head and trying to look tough.

"I ain't gonna spill nothin' unless I know your bud-
dies here'll go along," he snarled.

Jim took a swaggering half step forward and hitched
his thumbs in his belt. In a voice that he desperately
hoped sounded as tough as the other boy's, he cracked,
"We'll go along with anything Trix says. She's the boss
of this pack."

"Yeah, I thought that phony Bob-White stuff was
just a cover-up for your gang. Real high-class, ain't you?
Livin' rich and tryin' to steal a lousy grand from a
poor widow," he sneered.

"Cut the moralizing," Trixie snarled at him, "and get
on with your big deal."

"Okay, sister. It happens I need dough real bad. So
count out half of that loot for me and half for you, and
we'll both forget all about our little treasure hunt. I
won't squeal on you for stealin' the dough or breakin'
the buoy lights, and you won't squeal on me. Ain't that
fair enough?"

"Breaking the buoy lights!" Trixie cried. "What do
you mean?"

"Oh, knock off the innocent act, sister. Don't think
I ain't heard about you and the Coast Guard. You

can take the rap for that as well as me. I got plenty
of pals who'd swear they saw you bustin' them lights.
See?"

"Yeah, I see what you mean," Trixie said slowly,
smiling beguilingly at him. "Okay, let's count the
dough. Here, sit down on the floor so we can divvy it
up easier," she suggested as she plopped down right
in front of Jim and Brian. "You count it first, and then
I'll check it. Not that I don't trust you, you understand,"
she said. "And now that we're all such good pals, and
you seem to know *us*, how about telling us who *you*
are?"

"Why not? What harm'll it do?" he said with a trace
of a smile. "I'll be halfway across the country this time
tomorrow, and maybe by then I'll have a new name.
Who knows? Around here they call me Slim—Slim
Novarski."

As he talked, he knelt down near Trixie, ready to
count the money. As she had hoped, he found that
holding the revolver was something of a handicap in
untying the bundle, so he laid it down close beside
him. As he bent over the pile of bills, Trixie glanced
up at Jim and imperceptibly shook her head as she
sensed his plan to grab the gun.

"You know, Slim, you and I'd make a good team,"
Trixie said in a confidingly low voice. "You're smart.
How'd you get onto what we were doing?"

"Sure, I'm smart," Slim said, his face beginning to

light up, "but most folks don't think so. Like that Coast Guard outfit." He looked ugly again and after a short pause continued. "I could teach you a thing or two, Trix. You don't go around leavin' letters and charts where every Tom, Dick, and Harry can see 'em. Not when it means big money, you don't."

"Like when?" asked Trixie, pretending deep interest.

"Like when you and your pals had that fancy breakfast at Pete's place and left the letter lying out there on the table," he answered with a smug smile.

"How come you saw it? What were you doing around there?" Trixie asked, her eyes narrowing.

"Just checkin' up on you and your fancy friends. I got caught over here in the storm and couldn't get back to Greenpoint, so me and my pal slept over at the toolshed. When I couldn't get my outboard started, I decided to stick around and case this joint, just in case—" he said with a harsh laugh. "My pal got chicken and went home on the ferry next mornin', the bum!"

"You mean you slept in the shed for two nights?" Trixie asked.

"Yeah, all I had on me was a soggy sandwich—and no dough—so when I smelled that breakfast, I figured maybe I could sneak me somethin' to eat. No luck on the food, but I sure struck it rich when you blabbed about the hidden money!"

So it was Slim I heard that morning near the terrace, thought Trixie to herself, *and not a tame deer!*

"At first I figured all I had to do was keep an eye on you and let you do all the work, but then when Pete here got careless and left that copy of the chart in the shed, I said to myself, 'I'll have a go at this alone.'" Slim continued to count out the money slowly, stacking it into two piles in front of him as he talked. "That Pete, he ain't very smart, is he?" Slim asked, looking up at Trixie. He was getting friendlier by the moment.

"No, but he'll learn," Trixie readily agreed. "He's new at this game, you know." She gave Peter a condescending smile, and he squirmed appropriately at her pretended rebuke.

"What was that you were saying about the Coast Guard?" Trixie casually asked Slim.

"Oh, them!" he snorted. "When I quit school, I tried to join up with their outfit. I had to take a lot of crazy tests and talk to some of the big brass, and then they told me I wasn't Coast Guard material. Me, the best shot around here!" He spat the words out angrily.

"I should think the Coast Guard would have jumped at the chance of having a bright boy like you." Trixie beamed at him. "The way you can read a chart and all." She paused, hoping he'd rise to her bait.

"Yeah, that was pretty good, wasn't it? I got the jump on you that night when you was all hashin' it over on the porch, when you decided the chart didn't have anything to do with the sea."

"Where were you?" Trixie asked, taken completely

by surprise by what she had heard.

"I ain't never been very far away from you and your gang. You're a cinch to trail. I was hidin' in the bushes right by the side of the porch and heard the whole thing."

"How long have you been out here in the stable?" Trixie asked.

"I got here a little while before you barged in. When I heard your gang headin' for the smokehouse, I figured it wasn't healthy to hang around, so I scrammed out through the woods and hid up in the loft. I didn't know this was the end of that crazy course," he admitted. "It just seemed the best place to hide until I could figure out where you was headin'."

A Little Black Box · 17

By now Slim had completed the slow business of counting the money. The Bob-Whites and Peter watched him
without saying a word as he prepared to tie up the
two stacks of bills. They had amounted to exactly a
thousand dollars, in varying denominations. Finally Slim
sat back on his heels, his hands on his hips, gloating over
the treasure.

"A grand!" he gasped. "A whole grand! One thousand
beautiful bucks!"

He looked up at the faces around him, at Trixie, and
again at the money. Trixie, fearing he might try to get
away with both piles, slowly stood up and asked for
her half. She glanced at Jim and Brian, hoping against
hope they would see she was preparing for action. Slim
hesitated and then reluctantly handed up the money.
As she reached out to take it, Trixie kicked the gun on

the floor with all her strength and with her left hand, caught Slim by the wrist.

"Why, you dirty little double-crosser!" he screamed as he wrenched away, tipping her and sending her sprawling on the floor. Jim dived on top of him, giving Trixie a chance to recover her footing. Brian quickly retrieved the gun and hurled it as hard as he could through a window in the back of the barn.

"Pete, get Abe!" yelled Trixie, who was terror-stricken when she saw Slim land a blow on Jim's shoulder that sent him reeling backward. Both boys were fighting like tigers. Jim was barely able to recover his balance before Slim moved in on him again. But, although Slim was as quick and lithe as a cat, he was outmatched by Jim, whose training in boxing now stood him in good stead. Watching for an opening, Jim finally landed a right uppercut to Slim's jaw, sending him to his knees.

"Grab those halters," Trixie cried out to Mart as Brian and Jim fell on top of Slim, who was so groggy now that he offered no more resistance. They tied his hands together behind his back, and then, pushing him over, they put a second halter securely around his ankles.

"That'll hold you, you bum," Jim said as he stood up and brushed the dirt from his clothes. It was not until then that Trixie noticed an ugly swelling on Jim's forehead and that her own knees and hands were scraped raw where she had fallen on them.

"A fine pair we'll make going back to Sleepyside!" she said, managing a smile.

Honey and Di, the color drained from their tense faces, had felt completely helpless to do anything while the fight was going on. Now they insisted that Trixie and Jim get out of the dust-filled stable and into the fresh air. Trixie waited only long enough to pick up the money and the tin box before going outside.

"It does feel good to lie down," Jim conceded as he flung himself down on the grass. "How about you, Trixie? Are you okay?" he asked solicitously as she sat down near him and the others crowded around.

"Oh, sure. This isn't half as bad as the bumps I used to get when Honey was teaching me to ride," she chuckled, "but I *do* wish Abe would come. That character in there worries me."

"Don't worry about him. He's trussed up tighter than a Thanksgiving turkey," Mart said, glancing into the barn to make sure. He saw that all of Slim's bravado was gone, the fight in him expended, and he lay quietly, just looking up toward the loft as if to ask himself how he'd managed to land in this situation.

"You know, I can't help feeling sorry for him," Trixie said as she toyed with a blade of grass. "He's had two strikes against him from the start, because he's not very bright, you know."

"He sure isn't," Brian agreed, "but with the right kind

of training, he might have amounted to something. Don't you think so, Jim?"

"He's the sort I'd like to help in my school someday, but you should get them when they're young, before the wrong habits get set," Jim commented.

"What'll happen to him now? I wonder," mused Di, her eyes filling with pity. "He seems so—"

Her question was interrupted by the scream of a siren, and in a moment they saw the police car coming up the back road. "And here comes Peter with some man," cried Trixie, looking toward the house.

"What's this all about?" Abe asked as he came running up to them.

"Trixie always gets her man," Jim volunteered with a smile, "only this time it's a boy. Look in the stable." And they followed Abe inside.

He took one look at Slim, whistled softly, and pushed his cap to the back of his head. "Slim Novarski, isn't it?" he asked as he knelt down beside the boy.

"Yeah," Slim grunted. "So what?"

"The Greenpoint police are going to be very glad to see you, my friend," Abe said. "They've been looking for you for a week or more. You're suspected of stealing a powerboat, among other things. Am I right?"

"I don't know nothin' about no powerboat," Slim muttered, giving Abe a nasty look.

"Well, he knows plenty about the buoy lights," Trixie said, her eyes snapping, "and ask him if he's got a permit to carry a gun. I'll just bet he stole that, too."

"A gun!" Abe exclaimed. "Are you serious? Where is it?"

"Brian threw it out the back window after I—" Trixie hesitated.

"After she outsmarted Slim and got the gun away from him," Jim added proudly.

Peter, who had meanwhile come up to the edge of the circle, stepped forward and said, "Maybe we'd better begin at the beginning of this story. This is my dad, and he doesn't know anything about Slim or the letter. He just got home from Vermont this morning."

Mr. Kimball was a tall, well-built man with graying hair and an easy manner. His friendly remarks as he was being introduced made everyone feel a little more relaxed. Peter then suggested that Trixie tell about their adventure. She felt the color rising in her cheeks, but, encouraged by a smile from Jim, she recounted in detail the discovery of the letter and the subsequent search for the money. She avoided mentioning the fact that they had consulted Abe about it in the beginning.

No need to embarrass him, she thought, but when she was finished, Abe turned to Mr. Kimball and said, "If this had ended with somebody getting badly hurt, I'd have only myself to blame, sir. You see, Peter told me about the letter right after they found it, but I didn't take it seriously. How wrong can you be?" he added ruefully, shaking his head.

"Well, we won't worry about that now," Mr. Kimball assured him, "but I think we'd better do something about Slim. What's the procedure, Abe?"

"I'll just put these bracelets on him and take him over to the lockup in the town hall while I talk with the chief in Greenpoint and with the Coast Guard," he said as he took the handcuffs from his belt. "Will one of you see if you can find the gun? We'll need it for evidence, and later in the day, I'd like to get a deposition from you about Slim's confession."

As Brian dashed around back of the barn, Slim said, "I didn't confess nothin'. That dame there double-crossed me." He tossed his head in Trixie's direction and gave her a menacing look.

"Okay, okay, Slim. You'll have a chance to tell the judge all about it. How old are you, by the way?" Abe asked sharply.

"Seventeen, next fall," the boy mumbled. "What's it to you?"

"It's nothing to me," Abe replied in a more kindly voice, "but it may mean something to you. You're classed as a juvenile until you're eighteen, so your case will be heard in private in the Children's Court. If they find you guilty, there's a good chance you'll be sent to school instead of to prison."

"Who says school ain't prison?" Slim barked, and then, shaking his head as though confused by his own thoughts, he asked, "You mean one of them schools where you go to live and they learn you a trade or how to farm or somethin'?" He sounded faintly interested.

"That's what I mean," Abe answered and then waited for Slim's reaction.

"Gee, maybe that ain't such a bum idea. I wouldn't have to scrounge around for food no more. I'd have a place to flop at night, and. . . ." His voice trailed off into silence.

"Does your family live in Greenpoint?" Mr. Kimball asked him.

"Naw. My father died when I was a kid. Then me and my mother moved to Jersey. After that, she got jobs around waitin' on table, but she took sick last year, and they sent her to a hospital. I scrammed out, figurin' if I stuck around I'd only be a worry to her." Unexpected tears welled in the boy's eyes, and, turning to Abe, he said in a quiet voice, "Okay, let's get going."

By this time Brian had returned with the gun. He handed it over to Abe, who, after examining it closely, turned to Mr. Kimball and said, "I'm glad to say this thing isn't loaded, but I believe it takes the same kind of shells the Coast Guard picked up on top of one of the buoys. So I guess our hunt is over."

Mr. Kimball thanked Abe for his help and suggested that the whole affair be kept quiet for a day or so, until they determined who was the rightful owner of the money. Then he said, "Now, let's get back to the house, Son, and talk this thing over a little further."

He motioned for the Bob-Whites to join them, and together they walked slowly across the fields and through the gardens.

"I wish you'd take charge of the money," Trixie said to Mr. Kimball. "I'd feel safer if you would."

"Why can't we hide it in the little secret closet behind the paneling?" Honey suggested.

"That's as good a place as any," Peter's father agreed, "until you can give it to—what was her name?"

"Ethel, Ethel Hall," Trixie replied. "You see, when we went to see El, he told us about how Ed had been lost at sea and how his wife started a bakery. So we looked in the telephone book and found one in East-hampton called 'Ethel's Bakery,' and yesterday we went to see her and—" Trixie ran out of breath and laughingly threw up her hands.

Mr. Kimball shook his head as he said, "Well, I can see what Mother meant when she wrote me the Bob-Whites and Peter were keeping busy, but I guess she didn't know you were doing some sleuthing along with everything else. Now, to get back to Ethel," he continued. "Are you absolutely sure she's Ed's wife?"

"Oh, we *know* she is," they all cried at once.

"You must realize that when this story comes out, someone else may show up to claim the money," he explained, "so you have to have proof that will stand up in court."

"El could testify about Ed and Ethel, couldn't he?"

Peter asked. "He's known them both for years."

"Yes, that would help, but you still haven't proof that it was Ethel's husband who wrote the letter about the money."

"I have it!" Trixie exclaimed. "If we could show that the handwriting in the letter was really Ed's, wouldn't that be proof enough?"

"I should think so, but how do you propose to do it?" Mr. Kimball asked, smiling indulgently at Trixie.

"Well, when we were in the bakery yesterday talking to Mrs. Hall, she showed us a picture of her husband. Down on the bottom it said, 'To my dear Ethel, with love from Ed.' The writing was exactly the same neat backhand as the letter, and I'm sure there was the same little squiggle under both signatures."

"That's good enough proof in any court, I should think," Mr. Kimball said.

"You know, young Ed is coming home tomorrow," Trixie continued, her mind racing ahead. "Wouldn't it be fun to take the money over when he's there and surprise them?"

"We've got a perfect excuse for going," Brian put in. "You know, she asked me over to talk with Ed about medical school, and she invited all of you, too."

"Hey, wait a minute," Mart interrupted. "Have you perchance forgotten that we leave for home tomorrow?"

"Oh, we can fix that," Honey said. "I'll ask Miss Trask if we can't start back tomorrow afternoon instead, and

I know that when she hears about the money she'll say yes."

"Gleeps, Honey, that would be perfect," Trixie said. "We'll get packed this evening so we'll be all ready to take off."

"We'd better call Ethel and see if it's all right for us to go over tomorrow," Jim suggested. "Ed may not want a bunch of strangers descending on him, his first day home."

"Brian, you go call her while we're putting the box in the closet," Peter said as they went into the house. "There's a telephone in the library."

"And don't say a thing about the money," Trixie warned. "We want it to be a complete surprise."

Brian soon joined them in the sitting room to report that Mrs. Hall was delighted to hear they were coming over. "As a matter of fact, she insisted on our coming for lunch," he added. "When I started to protest that it would be lots of trouble for her, she said she wouldn't take no for an answer. She's going to pack a picnic lunch to take to the beach, so we'll have a chance to swim in the surf. Ed would love it, she knew. You know how she chatters!"

"I *hope* Ed will love it." Diana giggled. "He may have plans of his own, you know, and not want to be bothered with us."

"Only time will tell," Mart said philosophically. "I only hope Mrs. Hall doesn't forget my penchant for jelly doughnuts when she's packing the lunch."

"How *could* she forget," cried Trixie, "when your 'penchant,' as you call your unnatural craving, led you to buy two dozen of the things?"

"Only a dozen, dear sister. Don't exaggerate," Mart flung back.

Their friendly bickering was cut short by Jim's suggestion that they go down to see Abe and then have the rest of the day free to pack for the trip home.

Trixie's Tops! • 18

AFTER THANKING Mr. Kimball for his help and advice, the Bob-Whites drove with Peter to the town hall. They found Abe in the little office he dignified with the name "Police Headquarters." He was sitting with his feet up on an old rolltop desk, but as they came in, he sprang up and made a rather futile attempt to provide seats in the cramped room. It ended with Trixie and Honey sitting on the desk, Di in the one extra chair, and the boys squeezing on top of a filing cabinet and a small iron safe.

At Abe's request, Trixie repeated the story of Slim and the search for the money. She spoke slowly and thoughtfully to be sure she got the details right. Her deposition was taken on a tape recorder, and after listening to the playback, Trixie signed an affidavit that, to the best of her knowledge, it was a true statement.

"I'm glad *that's* over," she sighed. "I hope nothing I said will make it hard on Slim."

"He isn't such a bad kid," Abe remarked as he turned off the machine. "I've had quite a long talk with him, and I think he was scared to death and just trying to put on a big front."

"We all ended up being sorry for him," Trixie said, "especially when we heard what bad breaks he's had."

"Well, I've talked to the Greenpoint police and the Coast Guard, and just a little while ago I got in touch with the authorities in New Jersey where his mother lived," Abe continued. "This is the first time he's been in any kind of trouble, so the chances are ten to one he'll be sent to a training school or maybe to a foster home, where he'll have some real family life."

"That would be great," Mart said. "If only someone would accentuate the positive, Slim would be okay. He apparently knows a lot about boats and motors, and he said himself that he was a good shot, which isn't a bad skill if you use it right."

"Do you know what he said when I asked him what he'd like to be?" Abe asked them.

"A cop, maybe, or a fireman?" Trixie suggested. "That's what seems to fascinate most boys when they first start thinking about a career."

"No, you're way off," Abe said. "He wants to be a ferry pilot, and, you know, I bet he'd make a good one."

On the way back to The Moorings, Peter offered to

take his family's station wagon to Easthampton the next day, since Tom would probably be packing the Wheelers' cars for the return trip.

"Don't forget to bring the tin box with you," warned Trixie as they were separating for the night. "I think I'll take the letter and the chart, too," she added, "so Mrs. Hall and Ed can see how it all happened."

"We can hide the box until after lunch and then give it to Ed," Honey suggested, "that is, if we can manage to keep the secret that long."

Early the next morning, Trixie woke to find the sun shining brightly. She nudged Diana a couple of times to awaken her, and then the two of them went into the next room. Honey was still sleeping soundly and made mumbled protests at being disturbed, but she finally pulled herself out of bed, shaking her head to get fully awake.

"You two are perfectly horrible to disturb my dreams," she said drowsily. "I had just had an invitation to a dance from a tall, handsome man when you woke me up."

"Was he dark or light?" Diana asked her.

"Dark. He had black hair, and, come to think of it, he looked a lot like Brian," Honey replied with a smile.

"Sorry for the interruption, old dear, but your dreams will have to wait. Remember, this is the day when we make *Ed's* dreams come true," Trixie said. "Come on.

Let's get dressed. I heard the boys banging away upstairs ages ago."

As Celia was serving breakfast a short time later, the
phone rang. "I'll get it," Brian said, heading for the hall.
"It's probably Peter."

"Or Mrs. Hall," Trixie suggested, her face clouding.
"Maybe Di was right and Ed can't meet us."

Any fears the Bob-Whites may have had were
groundless, however, for Brian came back, smiling
broadly, to say the call was from Ed. "He wants us to
come over early because the surf conditions are 'Go,' "
he announced, "and he wants to be sure we'll have
plenty of time to swim before lunch."

"What a relief!" cried Trixie. "I didn't dare think
too much about today; so many things could have gone
wrong."

"Like the weather, for instance," Jim said. "Do you
realize we've had perfect weather every day since we
got here except for the first humdinger of a storm and
the early morning fog?"

"The weatherman probably feels so guilty about
throwing that storm at us, he's been trying to make up
for it ever since," Mart chuckled.

They got to the beach in Easthampton about ten
thirty and found Ed waiting for them at the entrance
to the parking lot. Trixie recognized him immediately
from the picture his mother had shown her. After
greeting him, she introduced Peter and the other Bob-

Whites. Ed had an easy manner, and, although he was older than they, he seemed genuinely interested in what they had been doing during their vacation. When they reached the bathhouse, everyone seemed to be talking at once.

They changed into their suits and then made their way across the warm sand to the edge of the water. At first sight of the long stretch of beach, the opalescent colors of big breakers, and the long view of blue ocean to the horizon, the Bob-Whites were speechless. Even Cobbett's Island, surrounded by the protecting waters of the bay, was nothing like this. They found it an awesome sight—even a little frightening.

Ed and Peter, who had swum many times in the surf, showed them how, by waiting until a wave was just at the point of breaking, they could dive through it. Honey was the first to catch on, and she made a beautiful shallow dive, disappeared for a few seconds beneath the breaker, and then bobbed up out beyond the combers. Mart was rolled over a couple of times before he got the knack of it. He pulled himself out of the undertow, his hair full of sand, undaunted and ready to go back for more tries. All of them improved with practice and soon were able to plow through the waves and swim out to calmer waters.

When they began to feel tired, they stretched out on the blankets Ed had brought, luxuriating in the warm sun, which soon dried their hair and suits. Brian and

Ed began to talk about medical school, and as Trixie listened, she nearly burst with suppressed excitement.

"I've been awfully lucky so far," Ed was saying, "what with scholarships and jobs, but, I swear, right now I can't see how I'll finish my last year unless I take time off for a full-time job."

"If you had it to do over again, would you still go in for medicine?" Brian asked him.

"I'd do it if it took me a lifetime," he replied. "To my mind, there's nothing like it, but be prepared for setbacks along the way."

Before long, Trixie caught sight of Mrs. Hall coming toward them, loaded down with two large hampers. The boys ran to help her as the girls shook the sand out of the blankets and got a place cleared for the lunch. Mrs. Hall, puffing from the exertion of walking through the shifting sand, greeted them cordially. "I've closed the shop for the day," she declared. "I figure that, with Ed home, I might as well take a real holiday and not worry about business. I do believe it's been over a year since I've had a day off, so I guess I deserve a vacation."

She began to unpack the baskets and to spread the paper plates and napkins on the blankets. Mart's eyes bulged as he surveyed the food. Two large Thermos jugs held piping hot baked beans with frankfurters cut up in them. There were containers of pickles, sliced tomatoes, and cucumbers, and for dessert, an incredible assortment of goodies, including jelly doughnuts. The exercise had made them all ravenous, and there was very little food left after they had eaten.

"I don't think I can ever move again," Trixie moaned. "I've never eaten so much before in my life."

"It's lucky we had our swim before lunch. It'll take hours to digest all we've eaten," Jim said.

"Well, while we're waiting, let's show Mrs. Hall and Ed what we found," suggested Trixie, trying to make her voice sound casual.

Everyone moved into a close circle as Trixie spoke, knowing the time had come to divulge the surprise. She took the letter out of her beach bag and handed it to Mrs. Hall. "Read this, and then we'll tell you all about it," she said, her eyes dancing.

"Why, this looks like my Ed's writing," said Mrs. Hall softly, adjusting her glasses and starting to read. "Oh, my goodness, what can this mean? A thousand dollars? Oh, Ed!"

"What are you talking about, Mother?" her son asked her, leaning over her shoulder to look at the letter. When he had finished reading it, he turned to Trixie, a puzzled expression on his face. "Where did this ever turn up?"

"We found it the first night we were at The Moorings," she explained. "It fell out of an old book."

"And because my sister is an incorrigible sleuth, she insisted on tracking down the leads until—" Mart was interrupted by a gasp from Mrs. Hall.

"Don't tell me she found the chart!" she exclaimed. "Why, I wouldn't have the faintest notion where to start looking for it."

"Trixie found the chart, and this, too!" Honey cried as she produced the black tin box from under the towel where it had been hidden. She handed it to Ed, who looked first at Trixie and then at his mother.

"Look inside," urged Jim. "Go ahead. Open it."

Mrs. Hall watched, the color draining from her face, as Ed slowly lifted the cover to reveal the money. No one said a word for a moment, until the reality of the situation finally struck home. Then Ed, putting his arm around his mother and drawing her close, said in a low voice, "Now I understand all you ever tried to tell me about my father."

Then the tension broke, and everyone started milling around, talking and laughing and telling about the many frustrations they had encountered before they found the money. Mrs. Hall kept saying over and over, "I can't believe it."

Ed, holding the box tightly, as though to reassure himself that it was real, tried his best to thank Trixie and the Bob-Whites.

"Honestly, we don't *need* any thanks," Trixie told him. "You don't know how much we all wanted to find it when we heard about your plans for next year."

"Trixie's right," Jim joined in. "Just knowing your

father's wishes finally worked out is enough for us. Now, come on, and I'll race you down the beach, if you can run with a thousand bucks under your arm."

The boys dashed off along the strip of hard sand near the water's edge. The girls helped to clean up the picnic things for Mrs. Hall, who was still so flustered that she nearly put the pickle bottle in Honey's beach bag.

"I don't think I'll get over this in a month of Sundays," she sighed. "Little did I know, when you walked into my shop, that all this would happen."

"And little did we know, when we left home, what our vacation was going to be like," added Trixie. "Remember, Honey, how I said I just wanted to sit on the beach and relax?"

"I certainly do! But do *you* remember I didn't take you seriously, Trix? I know you too well for that," Honey reminded her.

When the boys returned, everyone stretched out on the sand. Quiet descended on the little group, almost as though they were reluctant to break the spell of a wonderful day. Presently Mrs. Hall, who was nearest Trixie, leaned over and, gently patting her on the shoulder, said, "I hate to mention it, but as our sailor friends would say, 'The sun is well over the yardarm,' and I know you Bob-Whites have a long way to go."

"Good heavens, it's almost three o'clock!" Trixie exclaimed. "I can't believe it!"

Picnic things and towels were gathered up, and they made their way slowly back to the parking lot. Mrs. Hall gave each of the girls a warm kiss, saying she wished she'd had some daughters of her own. Ed shook hands with the Bob-Whites and elicited from Brian a promise to write him about his future plans. He waited to say good-bye to Trixie last, started to speak, and then, throwing up his hands, said, "What can I say, Trixie?"

Trixie felt the old telltale blush creeping into her cheeks, but Jim was there beside her to do the talking. "It *is* hard to tell Trixie what we think of her, isn't it, Ed? Let's just say she's tops."

Trixie dove into the station wagon, followed by the rest of the Bob-Whites, who laughingly began to chant, "She's the tops! Trixie's the tops!"

They waved to Ed and Mrs. Hall and then settled back for the drive to Cobbett's Island. Trixie voiced what they all felt when she said, "It'll be good to get home and see the family and our clubhouse again, but I don't think we'll ever forget this vacation. It's been perfect."